Star's Gift

Star's Gift

EMILY DEL ROSARIO

authorHOUSE®

AuthorHouse™
1663 Liberty Drive
Bloomington, IN 47403
www.authorhouse.com
Phone: 1-800-839-8640

Published by AuthorHouse   03/02/2015

ISBN: 978-1-4685-9465-2 (sc)
ISBN: 978-1-4685-9464-5 (e)

Library of Congress Control Number: 2012907443

Print information available on the last page.

Any people depicted in stock imagery provided by Thinkstock are models, and such images are being used for illustrative purposes only. Certain stock imagery © Thinkstock.

This book is printed on acid-free paper.

Contents

Dedication

To my Nana, I think about you every day.

I will never forget you.

Nunca te olvidare

A dreamer is one who only finds his way by moonlight, and his punishment is that he sees the dawn before the rest of the world.

Oscar Wilde

Prologue

AGOURA, CALIFORNIA
APRIL, 9ᵀᴴ 1994

She was born during the Spring Equinox on a night when the sky was covered with stars. The moon was in its last quarter. A light streaked across the universe like a flame at the moment she took her first breath. When her father first laid eyes on her, he kissed her rosy cheeks. As of that moment, their bond was sealed.

Her father announced that he would name her Star because she was like a little star that had fallen from the heavens.

However, his happiness would be short-lived. Not long after his infant daughter was born, his wife Madeline abandoned them without a word. This left her father, Stephan, to raise her on his own.

Stephan confided in his longtime friend Duncan O'Neal. Stephan and Duncan had attended the same law school. They became good friends and ended up working at the same law firm together. Stephan told Duncan he didn't know how he was going to raise the baby by himself. He also told Duncan he just couldn't see his little girl being taken care of by strangers.

A couple of days after they had that conversation, the doorbell at Stephan's house rang. When he opened it there stood Duncan alongside a little woman with a pleasant face and a wide smile. Duncan said to Stephan. "This is Inez Padilla. Inez, this is Stephan Serban. She is the answer to your prayers. Before you say anything, she is Lupe's cousin. You know Lupe, my housekeeper.

"Anyway, Inez has been here for about a year, working as a housekeeper. I hear she's a wonderful cook. She has her permanent resident card to work in this country. She's been attending night school once a week so that she can learn how to speak better English."

They all moved into the den and sat down.

"So Inez" asked Stephan, "where do you come from?"

In broken English, Inez said she was from Palenque, Mexico. She said that she came to this country to work so that she could send her mother a little money now and then. Then she asked Stephan if she could see the baby.

After Inez spent some time with Star, she told Stephan that she was the most beautiful baby she had ever seen.

Stephan said to Duncan, "You know I'm desperate, so I'll give her a try." Then he asked Inez when she could start to work for him?

"Right away," she said.

"You know, Inez, this is just a trial to see if you work out. What I mean is I want to see how you get along with the baby, and of course with me."

Things worked out well, and Inez stayed as part of the family. Inez loved the little girl as if she were her own. She made sure she got to school on time. She even took her to church with her every Sunday. Inez was like the mother Star never had.

Inez was a small lady in her late fifties, no taller than five feet. She always wore her hair in a braid rolled up into a bun. You never saw Inez without a smile on her face.

Star loved her daddy and Inez. She would often tell her daddy.

"daddy, you are handsomest Daddy in the whole neighborhood, in the whole wide world." Her daddy was certainly handsome; he stood six feet two inches, with reddish hair and green eyes, a gorgeous smile that made the women in the office melt whenever he smiled at them.

But Stephan never gave the women at the office a second look. His whole life consisted of work, and his daughter Star.

Star often wondered why she looked nothing like her daddy. She has thick light brown hair that fell past her shoulders in beautiful soft curls. Her skin was white like alabaster, her eyes were dark brown with thick lashes and a full mouth, and when she smiled at you she brightened up your whole day. Her daddy spoiled her like crazy. He covered the ceiling of her bedroom with fluorescent stars so that at night she would go to sleep looking at the stars.

There was only one thing he asked of Star and Inez: That they never go up to the attic. He told Inez he didn't want them up there because the floorboards were rotten. There was nothing up there, he said, but old furniture and a bunch of junk. "I've never had the time to go up there and get rid of all that stuff," he told her. Now and then Inez would catch Star at the top of the stairs, trying to open the attic door, but she never could manage to open it. Star would beg Inez not to tell her daddy, and Inez loved Star, so she covered for her.

Chapter 1

AGOURA, CALIFORNIA
2002

When Star was in elementary school, she was a good student. But she always felt different from the other kids and mostly kept to herself. She wondered why she was so different—why she knew when the phone was going to ring before it rang. She knew when someone was coming to visit without her daddy telling her.

She knew when something bad was going to happen in the neighborhood or in school before it happened.

When Star was in middle school, a group of girls tricked her at recess. They told her they had something to show her. They took her off school grounds. While two of them held her down, the others started beating her. They kicked her and punched her in the face. Then they all ran off, yelling, "Weirdo witch!" Star said nothing to her teachers or to her daddy about what had happened to her in school that day.

That evening she asked her daddy, "Why am I so different from the other kids?"

"You're not different, honey, you're just special," he answered.

After that incident in school, Star kept more to herself than ever. Her life consisted of her daddy and Inez. Her daddy always found time to take her to the movies on the weekends. Inez would take Star with her to the Spanish matinee during the week. Of course, when the circus came to town, her daddy would take her. Sometimes Uncle Duncan would go along with his girlfriend Renee.

Duncan O'Neal was a tall, lean, handsome man of Irish descent and a confirmed bachelor. He had honey-blond hair and sparkling-blue eyes. A week after Star was born he appointed himself Uncle Duncan.

Star was always happy when Renee came with them. Renee was her Uncle Duncan's new girlfriend. When she grew up, Star wanted wanted to be as beautiful as Renee. Renee was tall and blond and had the biggest blue eyes and the prettiest eyelashes, plus she was always nice to Star.

More than the circus, Star loved the carnivals. She always liked getting her fortune told by the gypsy. She also made sure she never left the carnival without buying some cotton candy.

Then one day when Star was about fourteen years old, she saw a teenage girl getting out of a taxi and moving several suit cases into Mrs. Rossi's house. Mrs. Rossi was their neighbor. She lived two houses down from them.

Star asked Inez about the girl.

"I don't know anything about her," said Inez.

"Why don't you ask Mrs. Rossi on Sunday, when you see her at *church?*"

Inez said she didn't want to sound like an *entremetida*—a busybody. But Star begged her and begged. Finally Inez said, "Bueno, bueno I'll do it."

When Sunday came around, Star couldn't wait for Mass to be over with. She kept looking around to see if Mrs. Rossi had brought the girl with her, but she only spotted Mrs. Rossi.

Mrs. Rossi was a lady in her late sixties with-salt-and pepper hair combed back into a bun. She wore a veil even though the ladies in the Catholic Church didn't have to wear them anymore. She had on a black-and-white polka-dot dress that came down to her ankles with big white buttons in the front.

Inez and Star caught up with her.

"Good morning, Mrs. Rossi," said Inez. "How are you this morning?"

"I'm just fine, and how are you, Inez?"

"Fine, fine. Star tells me she saw a young girl moving into your house the other day. Star is very happy to have some one close to her age nearby."

"Oh yes, that's my granddaughter Marie Ann. She's a little older than Star, she's almost seventeen. Why don't you and Star come over to the house and meet her?

"She's going to be living with me from now on," Mrs. Rossi went on, "The poor girl lost her parents last year. I'm sure she'll be glad to see a young person and so near besides her old grandma."

A couple of days later, Star and Inez knocked on Mrs. Rossi's door. A small slim redhead no taller than five feet, with green eyes and a pretty smile, answered the door.

"Hi," said Star. "We're your neighbors; we live two houses down the street. I'm Star and this is Inez, our housekeeper."

The girl smiled. "Hi. I'm Marie Ann. Come in, I live here with my grandmother now." All of a sudden her smile faded, and she said. "My parents were killed in a car accident about a year ago."

"We are so sorry about your parents," said Inez.

Mrs. Rossi came out of the kitchen, to meet them as they walked in. She motioned for Inez to join her, saying.

3

"I have something on the stove. Come in here and talk to me, Inez."

"Where have you been staying after your parents died?" Star asked Marie Ann.

"I was staying with my aunt and uncle in L.A. They didn't have a lot of room in their home. They have three kids of their own. My grandmother called and asked if I wanted to come and live with her. I jumped at the chance to leave that house. It was really crowded there. I'm sure they were relieved when I left."

"Are you going to Westlake High?" asked Star.

"No, I'm home-schooled."

"What's home-schooled?"

"It means I do my schoolwork at home. I'll be getting my high-school diploma in June."

"Cool."

"What is there to do around here?" asked Marie Ann.

"There's lots of things, we have a theater, a museum, a great mall. The beach isn't far from here. In March we have the biggest and coolest Renaissance faire."

"Oh, it looks like we have to leave. Come and visit me anytime if you want. That is when I'm not in school."

"All right I might just do that. Nice to meet you, Star."

"Nice to meet you too, Marie Ann."

Star and Inez left, and Star thought to herself how nice it would be if she and Marie Ann could become friends. That way she could have someone other than her daddy and Inez to talk to.

When they got home, Inez said "That poor girl, losing her parents like that and moving to a new place, not knowing anyone except for her grandmother. It must be hard for her. It must be hard for her grandmother. I think I'll light a candle for them Sunday when we go to church."

A couple of weeks later on a Saturday morning, the doorbell rang at Star's house. Inez answered the door.

It was Marie Ann. "I thought I'd take Star up on her offer and come and visit"

"Star you have company!" Yelled Inez!

Star came running down the stairs. When she saw that it was Marie Ann, her face lit up. The girls went upstairs to Star's bedroom.

After Marie Ann's visit, the girls became good friends. Even though Marie Ann was three years older than Star, they got along very well. Marie Ann became very fond of her younger friend.

Marie Ann was somewhat different herself. She never went anywhere without her tarot cards. She told Star that with a lot of practice, and if she got really good at reading the cards, one day she was going to Hollywood to read for the stars and become famous. Star would encourage her. "I'm sure you will"

"What do you want to be once you grow up?" asked Marie Ann.

"I don't know what I want to be yet," said Star. "When I was a little kid I wanted to be a movie star, but now I know that's not going to happen. Maybe I'll be a travel agent and travel all over the world. I like the thought of traveling."

"Well," said Marie Ann, "you still have three years till you graduate. As for me, as soon as I get my diploma from Westlake High, my grandma is giving me a check so that I can buy a car. That will be my birthday and graduation present."

"That is so cool! When's your birthday?"

"It's the twenty first of June."

"Can I go with you when you pick out your car?" asked Star excitedly.

"Sure as long as your dad takes us and helps me pick it out."

"Sure he will! My dad's great that way. After you get your car maybe my dad will let me go with you to the mall shopping for clothes or to the movies."

"I'm sure he will, but first I have to get my driver's license."

The girls visited back and forth. They tried makeup on each other, clothes, and jewelry. In addition, Marie Ann tried to learn how to drive, thanks to Stephan and Duncan, who occasionally gave her driving lessons on the weekends.

Marie Ann also practiced her tarot card reading on Star. Inez, for her part refused to have her cards read. She said that it was the devil's work. She would make the sign of the cross every time the girls sat in the den and laid out the tarot cards.

She even complained to Stephan about it. Stephan only laughed. "Inez, don't be so superstitious. They're not hurting anyone."

Inez would make the sign of the cross and stomp out of the room.

It would be a while before Star would find out how special she really was, for Star had the gift of premonition.

Life went on, with Stephan working at the law firm and spending time with Duncan at the golf course on Sunday mornings.

Now instead of taking Star places on the weekends, he had two girls to look after. He would drop the girls off at the mall or at the movies and pick them up at a later time.

They celebrated Christmas at Stephan and Star's house. Mrs. Rossi brought over her special Italian cannolis. They were Stephan's favorite dessert. She made them with whipped cream and maraschino cherries. Inez made bunuelos. "Everyone eats bunuelos on Christmas and New Year's in Mexico," she explained. "Bunuelos," she said, "were a thin tortilla; you deep-fry them and cover them with a certain kind of syrup called *piloncillo. The* syrup comes in cones; you have to dissolve them in a pan on the stove, and then cover the deep-fried tortilla with the syrup."

Duncan brought Irish dishes: spiced beef, braised cabbage, potatoes, and soda bread. "Wow Uncle Duncan," asked Star, "did you make all this?"

Duncan laughed. "Don't I wish. No, I ordered from an Irish restaurant."

"Where's Renee?" asked Star.

"She flew to Chicago to spend the holidays with her family. I decided to stay here and spend the holidays with my adopted family."

"Uncle Duncan, we're not your adopted family; we're you *real* family."

"Star's right," said Stephan. "You're a very important part of this family. I don't know what we would do without you."

"Well thank you, but enough with the mushy talk," said Duncan. "What else do we have to eat?"

"Besides Italian, Mexican, and Irish food we have American," said Stephan. "Inez, is that turkey ready yet?"

"I'll check on it," Inez replied.

"What about *our* ancestor's dish, Dad?" asked Star. "What country did they come from?"

Stephan looked at her nervously. "I'm not really sure," he said. "I'll have to do some research on that. We're representing America with the Turkey today."

Everyone laughed, Inez announced that the turkey was ready.

That day was a day that Stephan would never forget. He had his beautiful daughter with him. She was growing up so fast, and she was so beautiful. He had his best friend Duncan and he thanked God every day for Inez. Then there was Marie Ann, who seemed to be good for Star. At first he worried about the differences in their ages, but they got along so well, they were almost like sisters. Everything was right with the world.

Only one thing worried Stephan. He always hoped Star would never ask about her mother. What was he going to say to her if she ever asked about her? Hell, he didn't know what the hell happened to make Madeline leave the way she had, without even writing a note.

If Star ever asked about her mother, should he tell her the truth? The truth would hurt her that's why he had waited so long to tell her anything about her mother.

It was like yesterday when the police came to the door.

Star was only about a month old. They asked him to accompany them to the police morgue.

"There's a women by the name of Madeline Serban," said the young policeman. "I found this address on her," the young policeman said. "Alcohol and drugs were involved." He also said there was a man in the car with her, he was also killed.

As soon as Star turned eighteen, he would tell her about her heritage and her gift. That was all she had to know.

It seemed to Stephan that day was coming sooner than he wanted. He had tried to put it out of his mind all these years.

He had no idea what he was going to say to her. She already knew she was different, with the dreams and the premonitions she had as a child. Well, he would cross that bridge when he came to it.

Chapter 2

*I*n March Marie Ann got her driver's permit, thanks to Stephan and Duncan, who still took the time to give her driving lessons on the weekends. That meant that she could drive a car as long as there was a license driver in the car with her. The girls were constantly looking at car magazines, trying to figure out what kind of car would be best for Marie Ann to buy. She had no idea how much money her grandmother was going to give her when it came time for her to buy a car. She only knew that her parents had left a life-insurance policy for her. Her grandmother was in charge of the money until Marie Ann turned twenty-one.

In April, Marie Ann got her driver's license. Marie Ann still had two-and-a-half months before she would receive her diploma from Westlake High. She had finally decided on the kind of car she wanted and was hoping that her grandmother would give her the money to buy it. It was a red Pontiac Firebird convertible. There was one at the car lot by the mall priced at eight thousand dollars. She knew it was a lot of money, but she had fallen in love with the car.

On Sunday she went to church with her grandmother. She crossed her fingers behind her back and then lit a candle and prayed. "Please let my grandmother give me the money to buy the red Firebird." She hoped it wasn't a sin to ask for something as frivolous as a car.

On the first Sunday in May, Marie Ann and Star went to look at the car again. Afterwards Marie Ann couldn't wait any longer. She decided to talk to her grandmother about the car.

She sat her grandmother down and said, "Grandma I want to talk to you about something that's very important to me."

Her grandmother looked at her with a worried face.

"Grandma, I'm going to be getting my high-school diploma soon. You told me that when I did, I could have a car."

"Yes, I did say that."

"I found the car I want, and Grandma, I really want this car."

"What kind of a car is it?" asked her grandmother? Marie Ann thought to herself. *Oh, oh here it comes.* She's not going to go for it. "It's a red 2002 Pontiac Firebird convertible."

"How much does it cost?"

Marie Ann hesitated. "It's—well, I think it's about eight thousand."

Her grandmother was silent for a second or two. "Well," she said, "I guess that will be all right."

"What!" Marie Ann jumped up, and hugged and kissed her grandmother. "Oh my God! Oh my God! Grandma thank you, thank you! I have to go and tell Star, Stephan, and Inez." She ran out of the house and down the street.

She knocked twice and then opened the door and started yelling. "I'm getting my car! I'm getting my car!"

Inez came out of the kitchen. "What's going on?"

"I'm getting my car!"

Meanwhile, Stephan, had come out of his office, and Star came running down the stairs. "What is this I hear," asked Stephan. "You're getting your car?"

"Yes, my grandmother said I could have the Firebird, the red one."

"That is so cool! When?" said Star.

"I don't know, I forgot to ask, but who cares as long as I'm getting it!"

"Well, congratulations," said Stephan.

"Thank you, Mr. Serban."

"I told you before Marie Ann, call me Stephan. You make me feel like an old man when you call me Mr. Serban."

"Ok, Stephan."

Over the weekend the girls went to the car lot to look at the car again. Marie Ann asked the salesman if he could hold the car for her until the second week of June. She explained to him that she would be getting her diploma then. She also explained that she would have the money to pay for the car in cash.

The salesman told her that he would have to have at least a thousand dollars deposit and that he could only hold it for thirty days. She told the salesman she would be back.

"Well," said Marie Ann, "I'll have to tell my grandmother about this and hope she gives me the money for the car before I get my diploma."

"Good Luck," said Star. "Call me tomorrow and let me know what she tells you."

That night Marie Ann helped her grandmother cook dinner. After dinner she told her grandmother to go and watch TV, that she would finish up in the kitchen.

"All right, Marie Ann," said her grandmother, "what is it?"

"Well, Grandma, Star and I went to the car lot today. I asked if they could hold the car for me until the second week of June. The salesman told me they could only hold it for thirty days with a thousand dollars deposit."

Her grandmother was silent for a while. She stood up and walked over to the window. Then she turned around and said. "All right, Marie Ann, I'll give you a check so you can go and buy your car now." Then she quickly lifted her hand up. "Before you say anything, there are conditions. One! The first time you get a speeding ticket on that thing, you will park it for two months I know you already know how to ride the shuttle. You will also pay for the ticket with your own money.

"Also, Now that you are getting a car, you should start looking for a job or start thinking about attending college."

"I don't know about that, Grandma."

"At least think about it, will you, Marie Ann?"

"All right, Grandma. I'll think about it. Thank you for the car, I love you Grandma."

"Don't thank me. It's your money, you know."

"I know, but I still love you Grandma. I'm going over to tell Star, Stephan, and Inez."

"Don't stay out too late, Marie Ann."

"I won't." She ran out of the front door and down the street.

By now, Star was almost sixteen years old. She had grown into a real beauty. She was what is known as natural beauty.

She wore no make-up and had a mass of curls that came down almost to her waist.

One night, she and Marie Ann were sitting on the bed in her bedroom.

"I only have two more years before I graduate high school," said Star. "It seems like it's going to take forever, but with my grades, I could possibly graduate early. I can hardly wait to get out of that school. I had to be crazy to think I would meet a boy there and it would be love at first sight like in the movies. All the boys in that school are nerds. The cute ones go with the cheerleaders or the most popular girls."

"Those boys have got to be blind. You're so pretty, Star!"

"Not according to them."

Marie Ann looked at Star. "Look, Star. I'm going to tell you something I've never told anyone before. So promise me you won't say a word to anyone."

"I won't. I promise."

"When the right one comes along," said Marie Ann, "you'll know it. Love sometimes takes time. It's not always love at first sight. When it's love at first sight, you'll know it right away. You won't hear bells ringing or anything like that. You'll just know it. You can end up falling in love with a friend who you've known for a long time. On the other hand, you could bump into a stranger on the street and it could be love at first sight."

"How do you know all this? You don't even have a boyfriend yet."

"Well, I've read a lot of romance novels, and I also have some experience in that department."

"Tell me?" Star asked eagerly.

Marie Ann told Star a story about a boy she had met in L.A., before she came to Agoura. She told her that one day she had been on her way to the store on an errand for her aunt. She hadn't walked a block when she looked up and saw a boy coming towards her. He was tall and thin; that was all she could make out until he got closer to her. He looked down at her as he passed by and said hello to her and kept on walking.

"For me it was love at first sight," Marie Ann told Star. "I thought he was the cutest boy I had ever seen. He was at least six feet tall if not taller. He also looked like he was about twenty years old or maybe older. After that I had to find out who he was. I was obsessed with finding him. It took me three weeks and I finally did. Actually, it was by accident."

"I ran into him at the park one day, and we smiled at each other. He asked me to sit with him on one of the park benches.

We talked for a long time. He told me he was a part-time barber at one of the barber shops in town. He also said in his spare time he played the guitar with a group of friends a couple of times a week.

"He offered me a ride home on his motorcycle. When I got on, I had to put my arms around his waist to hold on and my heart was pounding so fast and so loud I thought he could feel it pounding against his back. When he dropped me off at home, he asked me if I would meet him at the movies Saturday night.

"That night he put his arms around me and when I felt his lips on mine, again my heart was pounding so fast I could hardly breathe. Star, I have never been kissed like that before. I thought I died and went to heaven. I had never been so happy in my life."

"So, what happened?"

"It didn't last long. We dated for a while, and then all of a sudden I didn't hear from him, he didn't call me. I didn't see him at the park or the movies or around town.

"Then one day, I bumped into him at the market. He smiled at me as if nothing had happened. He said. "Oh, hi, I've been meaning to call you. I have something to tell you. But first I have something for you." He held up a silver chain with a medal hanging at the end of it. He said it was a St. Christopher medal, and he hung it around my neck. He said, "I got this for you so that he can protect you." Then he said, "Marie Ann, I want you to know that I really like you a lot, but I have something to tell you."

"He told me that a girl in town was pregnant and that she had accused several boys in town of being the father, including him. Then he told me he had decided to marry her. I asked him, why are you marrying her if you're not sure if you're the father? Do you know what he said? He said *a man just knows.* Is that stupid or what?

"He never loved me, but I still haven't gotten over that jerk. I still love him. I guess I always will. Until I meet someone else and fall in love again, if that's possible."

"Why don't you read the cards? They might tell you when you'll meet someone else."

"I can't read the cards for myself, only for other people."

After Marie Ann left, Star thought to herself, *I hope I have better luck when I fall in love than poor Marie Ann.*

The night before Stephan was going to take Star and Marie Ann to pick up Marie Ann's new car, he waited until Inez and Star were asleep. He went up to the attic to retrieve an amulet that his grandmother had given him to give to his first-born girl child. He was saving it for Star but had forgotten all about it. But now that she was going to be riding in a car with an inexperienced driver, he would leave nothing to chance.

According to his grandmother, this amulet was a protection amulet. It would keep her safe on land, air, and sea. It would also protect her against illness and negative forces.

The next morning Stephan gave Star the amulet.

"Star," he said, "this amulet belonged to my grandmother. She asked me to give it to my first-born girl child. Star, I'm asking you, will you please wear it? It's a protection amulet; it would really make me feel better if you wore it. Please promise me you'll wear it?"

"Dad, is something wrong?" asked Star.

"No, honey, there's nothing wrong, just call me superstitious."

"Oh, all right, Dad I'll wear it. It's pretty. It looks kind of old."

"Yes, honey, it is old. It's an antique. The blue-green stones are turquoise, the light-blue stone is aquamarine, the black stone is tourmaline, and the clear stone is quartz. Take care of it, honey. Remember it belonged to my grandmother."

June was a very exciting month. Marie Ann got her high school diploma and was delighted with her new car. Duncan and his girlfriend Renee announced that they were engaged. Stephan decided to have them over for dinner to celebrate their engagement.

The evening of the engagement dinner, Stephan stood up and toasted to Duncan and Renee's happiness.

"Uncle Duncan," asked Star, "what made you want to get married after all these years?"

"Well, when Renee was gone at Christmas, I missed her so much I decided I didn't want to be without her ever again, and of course I love her very much."

"Oh, how romantic," said Marie Ann. "Now let's see that engagement ring."

"Well when's the wedding?" asked Stephan.

"We're not sure yet," Renee said. "I have to tell my family first. Then we have to set a date. Probably next spring, I have a lot to do. Like look for a wedding gown and pick my bridesmaids. I already know who I want for my maid of honor."

"Do we know her," asked Star.

"Yes, it's Norma Jean Cortez. My best friend, you remember her don't you Star?"

"Sort of, but it's been a long time since I've seen her."

"Anyway," said Renee. "I have to talk to the priest about a date for the wedding. Then there are the flowers, the invitations, and a hundred other little things."

"I'll help you, Renee," said Star.

"So will I," said Marie Ann.

"There you go," said Duncan. "You don't have anything to worry about now."

Renee looked at him and smiled. "Thank, you girls," she said. "I'll take you up on your offer."

"Uncle Duncan," asked Star, "is any of your family coming to the wedding?"

"Well, I talked to my cousin Mathew," said Duncan. "He said he was going to do his best to come. He also told me he wants to bring his son Patrick with him. I hope they can come. I haven't seen Mathew since we were kids. He lives in Ireland, you know."

"How old is his son?"

"Oh, let's see, I think he's about twenty-one or twenty-two"

"When are *you* getting married Stephan?" asked Marie Ann.

"When I find a girl as wonderful as my Star!" said Stephan.

Duncan laughed. "Well that'll never happen".

Everyone laughed, in agreement.

"Dad," said Star to Stephan after everyone had left. "Why haven't you gotten married yet? Is it because of me? Don't joke around, Dad. Tell me the truth."

"Well, Star, I just haven't found anyone I want to spend the rest of my life with yet. When and if I do, you will be the second person to know about it, I promise you."

"All right, Dad, but when I get married, what are you going to do here all alone?"

"I hope that won't be for a very long time. Besides, I have Inez, and I'm sure I can find something to entertain myself with, like maybe grandchildren."

"You're right, Dad, that won't be for a very long time." They both laughed and said goodnight.

*A*round this time, Marie Ann got a part-time job working for a young woman named Lorraine Day. Miss Day had just opened a small antique shop called Antiques and More on Agoura Road. Marie Ann told Star that she knew nothing about antiques but that Lorraine had told her that if she was serious about working for her, she would teach her what she could in her spare time. Marie Ann figured that at least she would eventually learn a little about antiques.

Marie Ann's job at the antique shop was to unpack the merchandise that came into the shop. She also had to make sure the place stayed neat and clean. She had to keep everything in the shop dust-free. Sometimes she had to assist customers when Lorraine was busy with others.

On Sunday, while Stephan and Duncan played golf, Renee spent the day at Star's house. They looked though bridal catalogues and magazines. They also talked about what kind of flowers Renee might want in the church, and the invitations.

Renee told Star, "my girlfriend Norma is going to be my maid of honor. How do you feel about being a bridesmaid?"

"Really? Renee I'd love to, thank you."

"That means you have to be fitted for a bridesmaid dress. We'll all get together once I decide the kind of dresses I want you girls to wear."

Renee liked spending time at Star and Stephan's house. It gave her a chance to eat Inez's delicious Mexican meals.

One afternoon when Star got home from school, Renee called her on the phone. She told her that she and Norma were going to a little bridal shop, in town called Beautiful Bride to look at wedding gowns. She asked her if she would like to come along with them. Star was delighted.

Before she left the house, she left a note on her dad's desk telling him she had gone with Renee to shop for wedding gowns. As they drove down Agoura Road, Star pointed out the antique shop where Marie Ann worked.

"We must stop and look at the shop on our way back," said Renee.

Once they got to the bridal shop, Renee tried on several gowns. Norma and Star tried to convince her that she looked beautiful in all of them.

Star thought to herself, how pretty Norma was. She looked a lot like the movie star, Eva Mendez. She had shoulder-length, dark brown hair, with reddish highlights and dark-brown eyes and she wore deep red lipstick. When she smiled she showed the deepest dimples.

Renee couldn't make up her mind. "You know what, girls," she said finally, "it's getting late. Let's just go for now. I know of another shop in Thousand Oaks. If you're free, Norma, we can go on the weekend or the next free evening you have, and of course you can come too, Star."

On the way back they stopped at Antiques and More. Since it was late in the evening, there was *only one customer* browsing in the store. A very friendly young blond greeted them at the door.

21

"Hello, I'm Lorraine Day, owner of this small and new establishment."

Renee introduced herself and Norma, and Star. "My young friend Star tells us you are employing another young friend of ours."

"Oh yes, you mean Marie Ann. She's in the back room unpacking merchandise. Come in and look around. You might find something you can't live without. I'll tell Marie Ann you're here." With a smile she turned and walked away.

Star couldn't get over all the beautiful things that were in the shop. Antique lamps, dolls, so many things. She walked over to look at the jewelry and the shiny music boxes. She knew they were old, but they looked new and were so beautiful.

She walked over to the counter and saw a pearl necklace. She put her hands on it just to touch it. All of a sudden she had this urge to close her eyes, and suddenly she saw a pretty woman. Her hair was stacked on top of her head in curls. She was dressed in a very old-fashioned gown, from the seventeenth or maybe the-eighteenth century. It was an off-white ball gown; the sleeves came down to her elbows and surrounded her arms with lace. From her waist the dress was lifted up by petticoats, and she was wearing the pearl necklace. Orchestra music played in the background.

All of a sudden, she heard Marie Ann's voice saying, "Star, are you all right?" She opened her eyes and took her hands off the necklace; she was back in the present.

"Yes, I'm fine, I was just daydreaming. What a nice shop."

"Yes, isn't it? I really like working here. Even though it's only three days a week, I'm glad you stopped by. I saw

Renee and Norma, they told me you guys were shopping for wedding gowns."

"That's right, but Renee didn't see anything she liked. Oh, I see Renee waving at me. We have to leave now. See you later!"

"See you later, Star".

Norma left the shop with a small lamp shaped like a rose with crystals hanging from the petals.

"Isn't it great?" said Norma.

Renee replied, "I knew you couldn't leave that shop without buying something."

Norma laughed. "I just can't help myself."

Renee and Norma dropped Star off at home. When she came in, her dad was in his office working. She walked into his office.

"Dad, I need to talk to you."

Stephan looked up at her. "What's wrong Star? You look like you just saw a ghost."

"I think I did."

"What?" Stephan stood up. "What happened?"

"Okay, on the way back from the bridal shop we stopped at the antique shop where Marie Ann works. We were all looking around the shop. I saw a pretty pearl necklace. I put my hands on it and went back in time."

"What do you mean, you went back in time?"

"Dad, I could see a woman. She was wearing the necklace and an old-fashioned gown. Dad, I could hear orchestra music in the background.

"Dad, is it starting again?"

"Is what starting again, Star?"

"You know what I'm talking about, Dad. Don't you remember when I was little, how I knew when things were going to happen?"

"Nevertheless, Star that hasn't happened in a long time. You know that."

"I know Dad, but this is different."

"Maybe you just imagined it, Star."

"I didn't imagine it Dad. What's wrong with me Dad?"

"Come here, honey." He took her in his arms and cradled her, just like when she was a little girl.

After Star went to bed he worried and wondered whether her powers, were growing already. *It was too soon, this wasn't supposed to happen. She was only supposed* to *have the power of premonition.*

From what she had told him, she had gone back to the past when she touched that object. Could she be an Empath too? He had read about them when he was doing research on people with premonitions. If he remembered correctly, an Empath is a person who is able to see events that have occurred years in the past at a given location, sometimes just by touching an object.

When Star was little, her problems were little. Now it looked like her problems were growing just like she was. He was going to have to find a way to keep her away from that antique shop. Marie Ann worked Mondays, Wednesdays, and Fridays. He had to figure out how to keep her away from that place on those days.

He agonized for days over what to do. Then he came up with a brilliant plan.

Norma owned and ran a beauty salon. He would call and ask her for a favor, and hopefully she would go along with it. He called Norma and asked her to meet him for lunch the next day. He told her he needed to talk to her about Star and that it was important.

Stephan got to the restaurant first. When Norma got there she asked. "What's going on, Stephan?"

"Let's order first, all right, Norma?"

They ordered their lunch.

"All right, Stephan, spit it out. What's going on?"

"Well, I don't know how to ask you, Norma. I need a favor. It's for Star, and I can't tell you why."

"All right, what's the favor?"

"I need you to give Star a job at your shop after school on Monday, Wednesdays, and Fridays. If you can't afford to pay her, I'll give you the money so you can pay her."

"What is it Stephan? You look awfully worried."

"I'm sorry, Norma. I just can't say any more than what I have already told you. I'm not trying to appear mysterious. I just can't tell you or anyone right now. Please, Norma be a friend."

"Oh, all right, I guess I can find something for her to do around the shop. Maybe I'll even give her a new haircut."

"Thanks, Norma. You're a sweetheart." "Yeah, that's what they all say. Have her come over to the shop after school on any of those days. I'll put her to work right away."

Stephan stood up and hugged her and kissed her on the cheek. "Norma, I'll never forget this."

That evening, Stephan sat on the sofa with Star.

"How would you like a job a few days a week after school?" he asked her.

"A job? Where, Dad, where?"

"Well, I was having lunch at a restaurant downtown today, when I ran into Norma. I asked her to join me. We got talking, and she told me she needed someone to help her around the shop."

"Really Dad? I'd love it."

"She only needs you three days a week, Star, and three or four hours a day after school. Do you think you can keep up with your studies and still work there?"

"Sure I can, Dad." "All right, then, why don't you call Norma and arrange a time when you can go over to the shop? If things work out, you can ride the shuttle to the shop and back home."

"All right, Dad. I'll do that."

That night Star went upstairs to call Marie Ann, and tell her the good news about her new job. Star told Marie Ann it wasn't in the bag yet, but she was sure she was going to get it.

"What are you going to be doing at Norma's shop?" asked Marie Ann.

"I don't know yet: all I know is that it will be extra money, a lot more than the allowance my Dad gives me now."

Stephan was happy now. It was much less likely that Star would ever go back to the antique shop again.

Norma gave Star a haircut the third week she worked there.

She told her that it was a gift for working so hard at the shop. Star had always worn her hair long, in beautiful, natural soft curls. "Once I'm through," said Norma, "you won't recognize yourself. You'll look so different. You'll look very mature with your hair a little shorter."

After Norma shampooed, and conditioned Star's hair, she sat Star on the chair. Star was so nervous; she had never worn her hair short before. She thought, *it's probably too late to jump up and say I've changed my mind.*

Especially, after Norma had given her this great job.

"How about I take about six inches off the back?" said Norma.

"Six inches, I don't know," Star quickly replied.

"All right, we'll just do four," said Norma. "I'll have to thin your hair out first. Boy, you have some head of hair. Do you know how many women would kill to have hair like yours?"

Star didn't say anything; she just sat there, petrified.

After Norma finished thinning out her hair, she started snipping. All of a sudden she saw her hair falling to the floor.

"I think I'll leave your hair a little longer in the front and shorter in the back," said Norma. "Then I'll give you some cute bangs."

Star thought, *Oh God what have I done.*

When Norma was done with Star, she removed the cape and turned her around so that she could see herself in the mirror.

Star almost didn't recognize herself. "Norma I love it," she said, "thank you so much." The girls in the shop all clapped and told her how great her new haircut looked.

Norma said, "with the wedding coming up you can show off your new hair style."

That evening when she got home, Inez saw her first. She put both her hands up to her cheeks, opened her mouth. She was about to say something, but Star quickly put her fingers up to her mouth. She wanted to surprise her dad with her new haircut.

Stephan was in his office, working as usual. Star walked in and cleared her throat. He looked up and said. "Well, who is this beautiful young lady?"

"Oh Dad, you like it?"

"Very much, except for one thing. You're just growing up too fast. I'm afraid I'm losing my little girl. She seems to be materializing into young woman before my eyes."

"Dad, I'll always be your little girl. You know that." She walked over to the desk and put her arms around him.

She walked into the kitchen to get something to eat. "What do you think of my haircut, Inez?"

"I think it looks beautiful. My little girl is growing up."

Inez started to wipe her tears with her apron.

Star hugged Inez, saying, "Don't cry, Inez. It's only a haircut."

"I know, but it wasn't that long ago that I was changing your diapers and rocking you to sleep."

"Oh, Inez, I love you."

Chapter 4

That night Star dreamed restlessly about clowns, a Ferris a wheel, a cotton-candy machine, and a gypsy. Marie Ann was also in her dream, crying. Star woke up with the feeling that something bad was about to happen. Not to her, but to Marie Ann.

What was that crazy dream about? Was her friend in danger? But, she couldn't tell Marie Ann; she would say it was just a dream.

She surely couldn't tell Marie Ann about the ability she had. How she could see the future in dreams. That the dreams she had only gave her hints of what was going to happen. She never knew exactly what or how, only that it would be something bad. If she told Marie Ann, she would think she was crazy. No, instead she would tell her dad.

The next morning, Star replayed the dream for Stephan. He thought for a while and then said, "I don't know what to tell you, Star. I wouldn't mention it to Marie Ann; maybe nothing will come of it. Whatever it is, you and I know you can't change the future. Just be there for her if anything happens. Hopefully, it was just a dream, honey."

"Okay, Dad I won't say anything to her."

After Star went to bed, that night Stephan felt really worried. Things were starting to happen again. First that thing at the antique shop, now the dream. How he wished his grandmother was here. He really needed her now.

During the week Stephan took time off work. He drove to the cemetery in Los Angeles where his grandmother was buried. He drove though the cemetery gates and stopped at the flower shop. He bought her white lilacs, her favorite flowers. He also picked up a map of the cemetery.

It had been a long time since he had been there. He drove around until he found the gravesite. He got out of the car and walked over to her grave. He felt a surge of guilt; probably because he hadn't been back to visit her since the day they had buried her.

He stood there a while. Then he said, "Grandma if you can hear me, I need your help with my daughter, Star. I don't know if I can handle what's coming by myself. If there are such things as spirit guides or guardian angels, she needs one now. God, Grandma, I miss you so much. I think about you every day." He set the flowers down by her headstone, turned, and left the cemetery.

That Sunday, Stephan and Duncan played golf as usual.

"What's wrong, buddy?" asked Duncan. "You've been distracted all morning."

"I'm just worried about Star; she's growing up so fast."

"I wouldn't worry. She's a good girl. I guess every father worries, especially when there's no mother around to help."

"It's not that. Inez has been just like a mother to Star. You're right. I'm probably worried about nothing."

"You know what," said Duncan, "Renee and I are going to the L.A County Fair. It starts in a couple of weeks. They have horse racing; you know how I love the races. Why don't you and Star come along with us and bring Marie Ann?"

"All right, I'll think about it," said Stephan.

Duncan dropped Stephan off in front of his house. Star was outside with Inez, watering the plants. She turned off the water hose and ran up to the car.

"Hi, Uncle Duncan, are you coming in for a while?"

"No, I have a date with Renee later on. I have to go home and spruce myself up before I pick her up."

"Oh, Uncle Duncan, you're so funny," laughed Star.

Duncan started to drive away, and then all of a sudden he stopped the car. "Star, you know, I was trying to talk your dad into going with me and Renee to the L.A. County Fair. You and Marie Ann are invited too."

Star turned and looked at her dad. "The fair? I don't know; I might be busy that day."

Duncan said, "How can you be busy? I don't remember telling you what day we were going. What's the matter, Star, are you afraid to ride on the Ferris wheel?"

The minute he said *Ferris wheel,* she knew she really didn't want to go. "No, I'm not afraid," she said quickly.

Just then Marie Ann walked up to the car. "What's going on?" she asked.

Star said quickly. "Nothing."

"What do you mean nothing;" said Duncan. "I'm trying to talk Stephan and Star into going to the L.A. County Fair with me and Renee. You're invited too, Marie Ann. Star doesn't seem to want to go. I think she's afraid to ride on the Ferris wheel."

"No, I'm not, Uncle Duncan."

"Come on, Star," said Marie Ann, "let's go. I love fairs. I can get my future read there by a real gypsy. You don't have to ride the Ferris wheel if you don't want to."

Frustrated, Star said again, "I'm not afraid to ride on the Ferris wheel. All right, I'll go!"

"How about you, Stephan?" asked Duncan?

"Yeah, I'm in."

"All right. I'll let you know what day we'll be going." He put the car in reverse, and off he went.

A couple of weeks later, on a Saturday, they all arrived at the L.A. County Fairgrounds. Stephan told Star they were going to the horse races. "If you girls need anything, call me on the cell phone. Also call me every now and then anyway. I want to know where you are."

"Dad, I'm not a little kid anymore," said Star.

"I know, Star, but look around. There's a bunch of low-life's around here."

"All right, Dad. I will."

"Your dad sure worries about you huh?" said Marie Ann.

"I know. It's because it's always just been me and him."

"It must be nice to have a dad who loves you so much."

"Yes it is, but sometimes he worries too much."

"What happened to your mother?"

"I really don't know. I don't think my dad wants to talk about her."

"Aren't you curious about her?"

"I am, but I don't want to hurt my dad by asking him about her. I'll probably get my courage up and ask him one of these days."

"Come on, Star, let's go get on the Ferris wheel. You're not really afraid, are you?"

"No, I'm not. Let's go."

They got in line. Star said, "I'm glad we came. They're going to have fireworks later on, after it gets dark."

After they got off the Ferris wheel, Marie Ann said "let's go and get a map of the fairgrounds, so we can find out where the gypsy fortune teller is. I want to get my cards read before we leave." They went to the information booth and picked up a map.

They soon found the fortune teller's tent, and Marie Ann walked into the tent with Star following closely behind.

"Who will be first?" The old gypsy asked.

"I will," Marie Ann said quickly.

The old gypsy motioned her with her hand to sit. Star stayed standing behind her.

The old gypsy asked Marie Ann if she had a question.

"No," replied Marie Ann. "I just want to get my cards read."

The old gypsy took the tarot cards in her left hand and a *talisman* in her right hand. The *talisman was round* with an outstretched hand, with symbols inscribed on it. It hung from a silver chain. She held the *talisman* over the cards and said, "I invoke the sacred elements to show us their wisdom and true path through these consecrated cards, so that we can achieve the ability to see the unseen." She then handed the cards to Marie Ann and told her, "Shuffle the cards until you feel like stopping. While you are shuffling the cards, think about why you are here and then cut the cards."

When Marie Ann had done this, the old gypsy did the spread, and studied the cards for a while. Then she turned over the first card.

"The reaping skeleton—the loss of a lover. It's time for the birth of something new or someone new. You need to let go of the past."

She turned over the second card. "Judgment. New possibilities are going to open up for you in the near future. You will get unexpected help from a stranger. There will be a change for the better."

Then, all of a sudden, she gathered up the cards.

"What's wrong?" asked Marie Ann. "Aren't you going to finish my reading?"

"The rest of it is meaningless" said the old gypsy. "You've had your heart broken in the past. It is interfering in your present life. You have to find a way to get over your broken heart. In the near future, you will meet a new man; he will help you get over your broken heart. At first, you will fight his romantic advances towards you. Don't resist too long, or you will lose a good thing."

The old gypsy put away her cards. "That will be ten dollars, please." Then the old gypsy looked at Star and said, "Don't be afraid of your gift. Embrace it, my dear".

Star stared at the old gypsy, and then they quickly walked out of the tent.

"I wonder what she meant by that?" said Marie Ann.

"I don't know. Do you believe what she told you?"

"I don't know. I want to. Wouldn't it be wonderful if I were to meet a new guy and fall in love again?"

They walked around the fairgrounds and played some of the games. They got on another ride and then decided to go and get something to eat. They were standing next to the cotton-candy booth, trying to decide what kind of food they should buy. A parade of clowns passed in front of them. Marie Ann laughed.

"Look, Star, aren't they funny?"

Then her whole body stiffened up and she looked like she was going to faint. She grabbed Star's hand and held it tightly.

"What's wrong?" asked Star.

Marie Ann didn't say a word. Then she finally said, "It's him".

"It's who?"

"It's him. It's Julian."

"Who's Julian?"

"Julian Charles."

"Who's Julian Charles?"

"Remember the story I told you about the boy I fell in love with in L.A.?"

"Oh. Did he see you?"

"Yes, he saw me. He looked right at me and kept on walking. He was with his wife, or at least I think it was his wife." Tears were streaming down Marie Ann's face. "That jerk," she said. "Just when I thought I was getting over him. God, I hate him."

"What did she look like?" asked Star. "Oh, I'm sorry. I shouldn't have asked you that."

"That's okay. She was pretty and she had big boobs."

"No wonder he married her. Not that yours aren't big. Oh, I shouldn't have said that either. Sorry."

Marie Ann wiped her tears. "Let's just forget about all this and have a little fun before we leave."

Later, Star told Stephan what had happened at the fair with Marie Ann and her ex-boyfriend. "You see, Dad, that dream did come true. Just like I dreamed—the Ferris wheel, the clowns, even the cotton-candy booth."

"All right, Star don't panic. If things are starting to happen just like when you were a child, there is nothing we can do about it. Honey, you can always talk to me, you know that."

"Dad, the old gypsy that read Marie Ann's cards told me not to be afraid of my gift, to embrace it. That old gypsy knew about me, Dad."

"Honey, don't worry, you'll never see that gypsy again. You worry too much. Forget all about this and concentrate on school and your job. Go out with Marie Ann, cheer up, go shopping, go to the movies, do girl things."

"Girl things—like what, Dad?"

"Oh, I don't know. Read each other's diaries, talk about boys."

"Dad, how do you know I have a diary?"

"Doesn't every teenage girl have one?"

"Oh, Dad, okay I'll try to forget about it for now."

"That's a good girl." He kissed her on the cheek and went into his office.

Weeks passed and nothing happened. Star didn't have any more dreams. Everything seemed to be going back to normal. It was time to concentrate on Renee and Duncan's wedding. Star and Marie Ann had made plans to meet Renee and Norma at a bridal shop in Thousand Oaks. Star was going to have a fitting for her bridesmaid dress. After the fitting, they all went to dinner at a restaurant close to the beach.

Renee and Norma talked about the wedding and marriage, and suddenly. Star announced, "If I ever get married, I want to get married in the spring, on the beach, just after sunset when there's a full moon and lots of stars in the sky. Also, my husband will be as handsome as a prince." The girls laughed.

"I already have my prince," said Renee.

"Oh, listen to her," said Norma, "just because she snagged a tall, blue-eyed Irishman."

"I went to a gypsy fortune teller and she said I would be meeting a man in the near future," said Marie Ann.

"When was this?" asked Renee?

"When we went to the L.A. County fair in September."

"Why didn't you say anything then? As I recall, you were kind of quiet on the ride home."

"I had a headache. That's why"

"How about you, Norma?" asked Star. "Where's your prince?"

"In hell, I hope! I divorced him a long time ago. You see, girls, my prince turned out to be an ugly toad. If I had the power, I would have turned him into a tiny little beetle and crushed him with my foot."

"Come on, Norma," said Renee. "Don't scare the girls."

"I'm not trying to scare them. I just want them to know you don't always get a prince. Sometimes you get a big fat ugly toad."

The next opportunity the girls had to get together in Star's bedroom, they both said at the same time, "Did you hear what Norma—" They started laughing.

"I wonder what her ex-husband did to deserve her wanting to turn him into a toad," said Marie Ann.

"And crush him with her foot," said Star.

"It was probably something bad. I bet he cheated on her.

Yep, that's what it was. You can't trust any man you know."

"They're not all that way. My Dad would never cheat on someone he loved, or Uncle Duncan."

"That's two out of billions of men in the world."

"Come on, Marie Ann, remember what the old gypsy said. You'll be meeting a new guy soon."

"Well, it better happen soon. Because if it doesn't, I'm going to find that old gypsy and demand my ten dollars back."

"What are you complaining about? You've already had one boyfriend, and you've got another one coming soon, according to the old gypsy. What about me? I haven't even had one yet, and I'm sixteen going on seventeen. By now I should at least have had one or two."

Marie Ann smiled. "Good things come to those who wait."

"Where did you hear that?"

"I don't know. Somewhere."

They laughed and passed the rest of the time evening inventing scenarios about Norma and her ex-husband and talking about boys.

Chapter 5

$\mathcal{J}$t was already February, and Renee and Duncan's wedding was approaching quickly. The wedding was set for the end of April.

One evening, Star got a frantic call from Renee.

"Star," she said, "I need your help."

"What's the matter, Renee?"

"One of my bridesmaids had to drop out. She just found out she's pregnant. The doctor wants her to stay in bed for the duration of the pregnancy. Do you think Marie Ann would take her place? The dress is already paid for. All that's needed are some alterations on the dress. What do you think, Star? Do you think she'll do it on such short notice?"

"I don't know. I can give you her number if you want to call her. She'll probably do it."

"Good. Give me her number. I'll call her and see if I can meet her at your house if that's okay with you?"

"Sure, that's okay."

The next evening Renee arrived at Star's house. Stephan came out of his office to asked her how the wedding plans were coming along.

"They were coming along just fine until one of my bridesmaids got pregnant and dropped out. Anyway, it's a long story."

Stephan smiled. "I'm sure things will work out."

Renee looked at him. "You know, Stephan, all you and Duncan have to worry about is picking up your kilts and putting them on. Oh, yes, and getting to the church on time."

"What about the honeymoon?" said Stephan. "From what I hear, Duncan planned the whole thing himself."

"That's true, only I don't know where we're going. He wants it to be a surprise."

"Really."

"Don't act like you don't know anything about it, Stephan. I know you know all about it."

"Okay, Duncan did say a little something about it, but I'm sworn to secrecy."

"All right, Stephan, I know you guys stick together."

Just then the doorbell rang. It was Marie Ann.

Stephan thought to himself, what luck I never thought she was going to let me off the hook.

"Hi, Stephan. I was supposed to meet Renee here this evening."

"Come on in. She's already here." He let her in and quickly went into his office and closed the door.

Star came out of the kitchen to greet Renee and Marie Ann. Star suggested they go into the den to talk. She said. "I'll go to the kitchen and bring some ice tea and cookies while you two talk" While Star was in the kitchen, Renee asked Marie Ann, "How would you like to do me a tremendous favor?"

"What's the favor?"

"Would you mind taking the place of one of my bridesmaids who had to drop out? I know that it's a last-minute thing the dress is already paid for. The only thing that you would have to buy is your shoes. If you can't afford to buy them, I'll pay for them. Oh, and the dress will have to be altered too—no charge either."

Without hesitation Marie Ann said, "Yes! I'll do it, and I'll buy my own shoes, Renee."

"Oh, Marie Ann, thank you so much, I don't know what I would have done if you had said no. This really puts my mind at ease, with all the other things I have to think about before the wedding."

By the time Star got back with the tray of iced tea and cookies, everything had been settled.

"I'm going to be in the wedding," said Marie Ann to Star. Star put the tray down, and they hugged.

"Who's going to be my partner in the wedding?" asked Marie Ann. "Oh that would be Patrick, Duncan's cousin's son," replied Renee.

"That means Uncle Duncan's cousin is coming all the way from Ireland for the wedding," said Star.

"That's right," said Renee. "Duncan is so excited about it. He hasn't seen his cousin Mathew since they were kids."

"Do you know what Patrick looks like asked Marie Ann?"

Renee laughed. "No, but I'm sure he's handsome. After all, he's an Irishman." They laughed. "Anyway, Marie Ann, I'll call you when I make an appointment with the seamstress to alter the dress for you. Plus, I have to show you the kind of shoes I want you to wear and where to get them."

That evening, after Marie Ann and Renee left, Stephan asked Star, "Honey, have you had any more of those dreams?"

"No, Dad, everything's been great. The last time I had a bad dream was before we went to the fair. Maybe it's because I've been so busy with school and working at Norma's and now Renee and Uncle Duncan's wedding."

"That's wonderful, honey. Maybe that was the end of those dreams."

"Dad, what about the antique shop and that pearl necklace?"

"Oh, honey, I thought you forgot all about that."

"Dad, it was so real I can't forget about it. I don't know how to explain it. You had to experience it yourself."

"Well, honey, all I can say is, try not to think about it so much. Oh, by the way, are you still wearing that amulet?"

"Yes, Dad, I'm still wearing it."

"Just checking, honey. You know how I worry about you."

In March the girls and Norma threw Renee a surprise bridal shower. With all this going on, Star still couldn't stop thinking about the pearl necklace and what had happened when she touched it. She made up her mind she had to go back to the antique shop. She wasn't going to tell her dad; he worried too much about her. She would go on a day when Marie Ann didn't work at the antique shop.

On a Tuesday, while her dad was at work, Star ditched school. She took the shuttle to the antique shop. When she got there, she stood outside the door of the shop, and took a deep breath before going in.

Lorraine immediately recognized her. "Aren't you Marie Ann's friend?"

"Yes, I was here once."

"Can I help you with something, or do you just want to look around?"

"I just want to look around, thank you."

"All right then, let me know if you need anything." Lorraine walked away to assist another customer.

Star looked around for a while, but she couldn't find the pearl necklace anywhere. Finally she asked Lorraine.

"The last time I was here, you had a beautiful pearl necklace over there on the counter?"

"Oh yes, I sold it to an elderly woman. She fell in love with it, and bought it right away. I have some very nice jewelry you can look at. I have them over there behind the glass case. If there's anything you want to see up close, I'll unlock the case and show them to you."

"I think I'll look around the shop some more."

"All right. Like I said, let me know if you need any help."

Star continued looking around the shop for a while, and then she spotted an old brass teapot. For some reason she was drawn to it. The teapot had a couple of dents on it. It wasn't fancy at all, it just looked like an old brass teapot.

She picked up the teapot and immediately felt an emotion like nothing she had ever felt before. She closed her eyes and was instantly transported to the countryside. It was almost dark; there was a full moon and there were people around a campfire. She noticed a woman walking toward the campfire, holding the teapot. She put the teapot on the fire. There was a gypsy wagon sitting under the trees. She heard violin music. She turned her head to see where the music was coming from, and she saw a man playing the violin.

The woman at the campfire checked on the teapot. She wore a shawl over her head and a long, colorful skirt; she had on a white blouse with brown drawstrings in the front. She had lots of bracelets on both arms and wore large earrings. Children were crying in the background.

Then Star heard Lorraine's voice behind her. "You like the teapot?"

Star opened her eyes and was immediately transported back to the present. "Yes, very much, how much is it?"

43

"It's only seventy five dollars because it has a couple of dents on it. It's a very old piece; I haven't been able to find out exactly how old it is. The person I bought it from told me it came from Romania or maybe Hungary. I don't have a certificate of authenticity for it. That's why I'm only selling it for seventy-five dollars."

"I don't have that much money on me right now, but I can come back Saturday and buy it. I have twenty dollars. Can you hold it for me until then?"

"I think I can do that. No one else has shown an interest in this old teapot."

"Good, then I'll be back on Saturday to pick it up. Oh, and would you please do me a favor? Don't tell Marie Ann I was here and that I bought anything. It's a surprise for a friend of ours."

"Don't worry. I won't say a word."

Star felt guilty about lying to Lorraine, but she felt she had no choice. She didn't want her dad to find out that she had come back to the antique shop. She surely didn't want him to find out she had bought something there.

On Saturday, Star took the first opportunity to leave the house. She got on the shuttle and headed to the antique shop. As soon as she got off the shuttle, her cell phone rang. It was her dad. Right away he asked, "Star, where are you? I had to go into the office to pick up some work. When I got home, Inez told me she had no idea where you were. You didn't leave a note like you always do."

"Sorry, Dad I forgot. I'm out shopping for a present for Renee."

"Didn't you already get her something when you girls had that shower for her?"

"Yes, but I wanted to get her a good-luck charm, so they can have a great honeymoon."

"They have good luck-charms for honeymoons?"

"Sure, Dad, haven't you heard of them?"

"Well, okay, be careful out there."

"Okay, Dad I will." *Great,* she thought now I *lied to my dad.*

When she got home, she tried to sneak in. Her dad heard her come in and came out of his office. "Hey, Star, what did you buy?"

"Nothing. I mean, I couldn't find what I was looking for, so I bought some underwear for myself." *Lie number three—will this day ever end?*

She went upstairs to her bedroom and took the teapot out of the bag. Lorraine had put it in a gift box for her. She would make sure there was no chance Inez would see it. She put it in her closet, and it stayed there for over a week. She started to take it out of the box several times, but every time, she stopped herself.

Finally, one night she took the teapot out of the box and she set it on the bed. She put her hands on it and closed her eyes. She was once again transported to the past. Again she saw the campfire and the gypsy wagon. She could hear violin music nearby. This time people were dancing around the campfire. She saw a woman holding the teapot, walking over to a small table. She poured whatever liquid was in the teapot into some small cups. Then she heard a knock at the door.

"Star, are you in there? It's me, Marie Ann. Why is your door locked?"

Star immediately returned to the present. "Just a minute. I'll be right there."

She quickly put the teapot in the box and shoved it into the closet. She opened the door for Marie Ann.

"How come your door was locked?"

"It must have gotten locked by accident."

"So what have you been up to?" asked Marie Ann.

"Why"

"No reason. Just asking. What's wrong, Star? You sure are acting strange."

"There's nothing wrong. How about you? How's work?"

"Fine. I'm excited about the wedding!"

"So am I."

After Marie Ann left, she decided to leave the teapot alone for a while. She was beginning to think it was bad luck. She had lied to three people because of that teapot. She was going to concentrate on school, her job, and the wedding. She was going to put that teapot out of her mind for now.

The next day she called Marie Ann and asked her to go shopping with her on Saturday. She told her she wanted to buy Renee a good luck-charm to take on her honeymoon.

"Sure," said Marie Ann, "that should be fun. I don't have anything to do on Saturday."

"How about eleven o'clock?" said Star. "That way we can have lunch at the mall first and then go shopping."

"Okay, I'll be ready. Why don't you walk over to my house and we can leave from here?"

"All right. I'll see you then."

The next morning, Inez yelled for Star. That Renee was on the phone.

"Hi, Star," said Renee. "The dresses are ready and the seamstress would like you and Marie Ann to pick them up by Saturday morning."

"I think we can do that. I'll call Marie Ann and tell her."

"That's great. I'll give her a call and tell her you'll be there Saturday morning to pick them up."

The wedding was in two weeks, and Marie Ann was still curious about her partner.

"When are Duncan's cousin and his son arriving from Ireland?" she asked Star.

"I don't know. I have to ask my dad."

"I sure hope he's cute."

"I'm sure he is. Don't you remember what Renee said?"

"What did she say?"

"She said something like, of course he's good-looking he's an Irishman, isn't he?"

Marie Ann laughed.

Star said, "Well, you'll just have to wait until the day of the wedding rehearsal. It'll be a surprise."

"I hate surprises."

"Oh come on, Marie Ann, it's only for that one day. It's not like you're going to marry him or anything like that."

"Yeah, I guess you're right."

It was a week before the wedding, and Marie Ann had just picked up the shoes that she was going to wear the day of the wedding. It was pouring rain, and the wind was blowing hard. The sky was thundering, and lightning crashed across the sky.

Marie Ann parked her car in front of her house and locked it. She started to walk up towards the sidewalk that led to her house, but slipped and fell on some wet leaves, right on her behind. The box with the shoes inside went flying out of her hands. All of a sudden she felt someone trying to pick her up. She looked up and saw a strange man.

"Let go of me. I can get up be myself!" she said to him. He bent over and picked up the box the shoes were in and handed it to her.

"I was just trying to help you," he said.

She was furious because he had seen her fall on her behind. Especially someone she didn't even know. "I don't need any help, thank you very much. I can get up by myself. Who are you anyway? What are you doing around here? I know you don't live in this neighborhood."

"I'm from out of town. I'm visiting relatives—."

She didn't let him finish his sentence. She grabbed the box from him without even thanking him, and hurried into the house.

She got on the phone and called Star.

"Star, I think I just met Duncan's Cousin's son Patrick."

"Really, when, where, tell me?"

"It's a long story, but I was so rude to him. I didn't realize who he was until I got in the house."

Marie Ann told Star everything that happened with Patrick.

"Maybe it wasn't Patrick."

"It was him."

"You sound so sure".

"I know it was him, he had an Irish accent. God, I hope he's not my partner for the wedding procession." said Marie Ann.

Chapter 6

The next evening was the wedding rehearsal at the church.

Marie Ann rode to the church with Stephan and Star. On the way to the church she told them all about what had happened the night before.

"Stephan, I'm so embarrassed about what happened last night. What if it was Patrick O'Neal? Marie Ann almost shouted.

"Don't worry about it." said. Stephan.

"That's what I told her, Dad," said Star.

As soon as they entered the church, Marie Ann saw him. "There he is," she whispered to Stephan.

"Who?"

"The guy I told you about, the guy I saw last night by my house."

"You mean the one you thought was Patrick O'Neal. The one you were so mean to."

"Yes, that's him." Stephan laughed out loud.

"What's so funny?" asked. Marie Ann.

Once Stephan stopped laughing, he said, "The guy you were so mean to last night is Patrick O'Neal, your partner in the wedding procession."

"Oh my God, I knew it. I feel like a fool. Oh, God, he's my partner."

"Come on, I'll introduce you to him."

"Hey, Patrick, this is Marie Ann. She's one of the brides maids and your partner in the wedding procession. I hear you two already know each other." With a big smile he walked away.

Marie Ann looked at Patrick and said. "I am so sorry about last night. I didn't realize who you were."

"I tried to explain."

"I know you did, again I'm sorry."

"All right. Let's pretend like we just met tonight for the first time."

All of a sudden Marie Ann *remembered* the gypsy's words. *A new man, don't resist him or you will lose a good thing.* Could he be the new man in her life? He was certainly good-looking, that was for sure.

"Marie Ann are you all right?" he asked.

"Hi my name is Marie Ann," she said.

"I'm Patrick,"

They laughed.

Finally the day of the wedding was here. Star was so excited. This was the first time she was going to be in a wedding and the first time being a bridesmaid. She just loved her bridesmaids dress. She said to Marie Ann, "Too bad we can only wear these pretty dresses only once. I really like them."

"Yes, they are pretty, aren't they? Renee has good taste."

Marie Ann, Star, and Mrs. Rossi were riding to the church together. Inez had decided to stay home; she said if the day ever came when Stephan or Star got married, then she would attend. There was no changing her mind. On the way out Inez said to them. "You all look so pretty. You too, Stephan."

When they arrived at the church, Renee and Norma were already there. The girls ran up to Renee and hugged her. They both said in unison. "You look so beautiful," Norma was helping Renee with the finishing touches, such as straightening out her green Irish sash and her veil.

"So how are you and your Irish stranger getting along?" Star asked Marie Ann.

"Very funny, Star. We're getting along just fine. We decided to pretend like we just met for the first time the night of the rehearsal."

"Oh, *really?*"

"Don't say Oh really that way. There's nothing going on."

"Okay, okay."

"Let's just forget about him and concentrate on the wedding," said Marie Ann.

Norma said, "I just saw Duncan. He looked so handsome in his kilt. So does Duncan's Irish cousin and his son Patrick. Aren't they some pretty eye candy?"

"What about my dad?" asked Star.

"Of course," said Norma. "I've always thought Stephan was a hunk, he just never gave me a second look. He sees me only as a friend." Star and Marie Ann threw each other a look.

Just then the door opened. It was one of the other bridesmaids. "It's time, girls," she said. "Let's get this show on the road."

Norma got Renee's bouquet and straightened out her veil.

The girls picked up their bouquets. Just then, Renee's father walked in. "Ready, dear?" "Ready, Dad."

Everyone left the room except for Renee and her father.

The girls all wished Renee luck. They also said goodbye to Mr. Murray, Renee's Father.

The pianist started playing "*Canon in F*". Duncan and Stephan were standing at the altar, with the groomsmen standing nearby. Norma thought to herself as she saw Stephan standing at the altar that he looked so handsome in his kilt and his green cummerbund and tie. Then she said to herself. *Stop it, Norma, what are you doing?*

Then it was time for the procession of bridesmaids. It would start with the maid of honor last, then the ring bearer, and, then the flower girl. The music stopped for a couple of minutes, then started again, playing "Here comes the bride." Renee walked down the aisle on her father's arm, looking so beautiful, just like a bride should. Everyone stood up and turned to look at the beautiful bride.

After the priest pronounced them husband and wife, everyone clapped. The music started playing again, and husband and wife walked down the aisle to the sounds of bagpipe music. The best man and maid of honor walked behind them, followed by the procession of bridesmaids and groomsmen.

The reception was wonderful. Star had the opportunity to meet new boys her own age who didn't attend her school. She had never had such a good time. She met a boy named Rudy Linarez. He just came up to her and introduced himself.

"Hi, my name is Rudy. I see you're one of the bridesmaids."

"Yes, I'm Star Serban."

"Is Stephan your father?"

"Yes he is, why?"

"My father plays golf with your father and Duncan sometimes."

"Well, it was nice meeting you. It's getting late. I have to go and help Renee put the gifts in the van."

"Will I see you at the dance tonight?"

"Yes I'll be there."

The dance was at eight, and Star couldn't wait. When she saw Marie Ann at the house, she told her she had met a boy at the reception.

"Oh, do tell!"

"His name is Rudy Linarez."

"Tell me all about him."

"Well, he's about six feet tall with the dreamiest green eyes you have ever seen. He also has light-brown wavy hair and a smile that will knock you off your feet. His father is an attorney and plays golf with Dad and Uncle Duncan sometimes."

"How old is he?"

"I'm not sure. I think he's a little bit older than I am. We didn't get a chance to talk too much. I can hardly wait until the dance tonight. How about you, do you like Patrick?"

"Yes, actually I do. How could I not like him, he's got that sexy Irish accent. He's tall he has a great tan and that sun-streaked hair that almost reaches his collar, is a turn on for me. Not to mention those gorgeous brown eyes and those lips.

What are you smiling about?"

"Because, maybe we'll finally both get a boyfriend."

"Maybe *you* will, but Patrick will be going back to Ireland once this is all over."

"Oh, I forgot about that. Well, try to have as much fun as you can with him as long as he's here."

They arrived at the dance. The music was playing, and the place looked like something in a fantasy. There were tiny lights wrapped around the posts. Icicle lights hung from the ceiling and the hall was dimly lit. The dance floor was in the middle of the room. Round tables with white tablecloths and green napkins were pushed against the walls. Each table had wine flutes and a beautiful centerpiece on each one. The bride and groom were seated at the head of an eight-foot banquet table accompanied by the best man and maid of honor.

Star looked around for Rudy. She didn't see him. Maybe he wasn't there yet, she thought.

Patrick came over and asked Marie Ann to dance. Star stood there for a while, and then she decided to take a walk outside in the garden. The air was alive with the fragrance of spring flowers. She looked up at the sky to see a full moon. She wondered when Rudy would show up. Would he ask her to dance, would he ask her to walk with him in the garden? Would he kiss her?

What was wrong with her? Why was she imagining all these things? She had just met the guy once. Could it be love at first sight, like Marie Ann had told her? She decided to go back inside. She walked over to the punch bowl and poured herself a cup of punch. Then she heard his voice behind her.

"Why don't you pour me one too?" he said.

Her heart was racing. How could she feel like this about someone she had just met? "Sure, take this one," she told him.

Then she turned and poured herself a cup.

"I looked for you on the dance floor," said Rudy. "I saw Marie Ann and your father. For a while I thought maybe you decided not to come."

"I was out in the garden looking at the flowers, I love their scent. They're at their best in the spring, you know."

"It's a beautiful night out. Why don't we go and enjoy those flowers together?"

"All right." She surprised herself with how fast she answered him.

They walked out to the garden. The night was glorious.

"It's nice out here," he said. "No wonder you like it out here. Look at those stars. If we stay out here long enough we might see a falling star. Then we can make a wish on it together."

"If we stay out here too long my dad will wonder where I am."

"Just a few minutes more, Star. Tell me a little bit about yourself?"

"Well, I live here in Agoura with my dad and our house keeper, Inez, who raised me. Inez is like a mother to me. She has taken care of me since right after I was born."

"What happened to your mother?"

"That's a mystery. I really don't know. My dad doesn't seem to want to talk about her. I've come to the conclusion that she's not dead, because if she was, he would have said something to me a long time ago."

"What do you think happened?"

"I don't know, but I'm going to ask my dad as soon as I get my courage up. I don't know why I'm telling you all this? I hardly know you."

"Sometimes it's easier to tell a stranger your problems than someone you know very well."

"Maybe you're right. How about you? I don't know anything except that your father knows my Dad and Uncle Duncan."

"Well, my father wanted me to become an attorney just like him. It just wasn't for me, so I broke his heart and decided to become an architect."

55

"What kind of architect?"

"I'm studying building design."

"How long have you been in college?"

"I've been going to the University of San Francisco for three years now."

"How much longer do you have to go before you get your degree?"

"Two more years."

"How old are you?"

"That's a lot of questions."

"Well—how old are you?"

"I'm twenty one and you?"

"I'll be eighteen soon."

"Oh, that's good."

They walked over to where the water fountain was and put their cups down. They looked up at the sky, hoping to see a falling star. All of a sudden, he put his arms around her and slowly brought his mouth to hers. It came as such a shock to her, even though this was what she wanted. Her heart was pounding loud and hard, but she couldn't move. Her eyes were wide opened.

He let her go and asked. "Is something wrong, Star?"

"No, there's nothing wrong, but there is something I have to tell you. You're the first one. What I mean is that you're the first boy who has ever kissed me."

He stared at her for a minute not knowing how to reply to what he had just heard her say. "Star, I can't believe as beautiful as you are and as old as you are—do you mean to tell me that you haven't had any boyfriends yet?"

"Like I said, you're the first."

"Wow, I really feel special, a beautiful girl like you and to have me be the first. I've never been anybody's first. Where have you been, in a convent?"

"Are you making fun of me?"

"No, I just can't believe such a beautiful girl like you hasn't had a boyfriend yet."

"I just never found anyone I liked enough until now."

"Can I kiss you again? I'll be gentle with you, Star."

"Yes, you can kiss me again."

Before the night was over, Rudy and Star exchanged phone numbers. He promised to call her as often as he could. He told her he would be home for the holidays to see her. "I'm going to miss you, Star," he said to her before they parted and kissed her one more time, long and tenderly.

On Wednesday Marie Ann came over to Star's after dinner.

"Why don't we go up to your room and talk?" said Marie Ann.

"So what's going on, Star?"

"Not much. Why?"

"Don't give me that. I saw you and that guy Rudy in a lip-lock out in the garden at the dance."

"I don't want my dad to find out"

"So tell me all about it?"

"Well, we were just walking out there and he kissed me."

"Just like that."

"Well, no, after he kissed me the first time, I told him he was the first boy I had ever kissed."

"You didn't. What did he say?"

"He thought it was great. We exchanged numbers and he said he was going to call me as often as he could. On his holiday breaks, he said I'll be the first one he'll call to let me know when he was coming home."

"Where does he go to school?"

"He's going to the University of San Francisco."

"How old is this guy?"

"He's twenty-one."

"He's a little old for you, isn't he?"

"No, he's not!"

"Boy, you really like him, don't you?"

"Yeah, I really do, but I lied to him about my age. I told him I was almost eighteen."

"Star!"

"Well, I will be soon."

"Not until next year!" Marie Ann practically shouted.

"All right, all right by the time he comes home I *will* be almost eighteen."

"You better hope so, and you better hope your dad doesn't find out."

"What about you and Patrick? You haven't said a word about him?"

"I never thought I would meet someone who would make me forget that jerk. God, I can't even remember his name now. Oh yea—Julian, that jerk."

"When is he going back to Ireland?"

"He's here on a thirty-day visa. His father left yesterday. Patrick will be staying for another two weeks. He's staying in Duncan's old apartment."

"All this has happened and you haven't told me."

"I've been trying to spend as much time with Patrick as possible. We only have two weeks to be with each other."

"So you two like each other?"

"Yes, very much. Star, I think I'm falling in love with him. I didn't think it could happen again, and so soon, but it has. I know I just met him, but I feel in my heart he's the one for me."

"Just like the gypsy said, remember." Star reminded her.

"What am I going to do when he goes back to Ireland?"

"Gosh, I don't know. I'm really sorry."

After Marie Ann left, Star wondered how many secrets she could keep. She was hiding the teapot and now she was hiding Rudy from her dad. She didn't want to lose Rudy; she really liked him.

He was so handsome and nice and such a good kisser. Not that she had anyone to compare him to. So what? It felt wonderful when he kissed her; that was all that mattered to her. It wasn't just the kisses; it was the way he looked at her. When he looked at her it made her feel like she was the only girl in the room, the only girl in the world. She felt like she could wait for him forever. Good thing she had only given him her cellphone number. There would be no chance that Inez or her dad would know that a boy was calling her. The minute they found out, they would want to know who he was.

That night she went to bed hoping to dream about Rudy.

Instead she dreamed about violins and gypsy caravans. In her dream she saw a man driving a gypsy wagon in the countryside. A women was sitting next to him. She looked like she was in her sixties and had a beautiful smile. She had long brown wavy hair, and wore big earrings and a pendant around her neck—a crescent-moon pendant. She turned and looked at Star and said, "Don't reject your gift my dear, embrace it." Star suddenly realized that the woman resembled her. Then she woke out of her dream.

She wondered if it could have been one of her ancestors trying to give her a message, just like the gypsy.

The next morning Star asked her dad if he had any pictures of his family.

"Why are you interested in old pictures of the family all of a sudden?" he asked.

"We're studying genealogy in school." she lied.

"Oh, well, as soon as I get the time I'll dig them up for you."

"Can you do it by this weekend, Dad, please?"

"All right, honey, I'll do it."

Stephan thought, *great*. He had known this day was coming.

Well there was nothing he could do about it now but wait and see what happened from now on.

Chapter 7

*B*efore the weekend came around Stephan went to the attic to retrieve some photos that belonged to his grandmother. He would have to choose certain ones. He wasn't ready to tell Star about her heritage just yet. Bad enough she had to deal with her so-called gift and her dreams.

He would give everything he had in the world for her to grow up to be a normal person, but her destiny was set and there was nothing they could do about it. Either she was going to be happy and accept what she was, or she was going to live a very sad life trying to deny it.

Meanwhile, Marie Ann and Patrick were spending as much time with each other as possible. She invited him over to dinner a couple of times. She wanted her grandmother to get to know him.

Mrs. Rossi asked him what kind of work he did in Ireland.

"My family owns and runs a small tourist business in Union Hall, in County Cork. It's a small fishing village. My two brothers, Aiden and Conner, and I help my father run it. We own a few fishing boats. We take tourists out for a day's fishing. My mother and younger brother Devin take care of the tackle shop; they also sell soft drinks and such. That's one of the reasons why I can't stay here any longer. My father needs me to come home and help him with the fishing boats. Right now my cousin Finn is helping my father out with the boats."

"Well, we're going to hate to see you go. You seem like a real nice boy. I know my Marie Ann likes you a lot."

"Grandma!" Marie Ann said loudly.

"Always tell the truth, Marie Ann, never hide your feelings. I'll leave you two young people alone to talk. Good night."

"Good night, Mrs. Rossi."

"Good night, Patrick."

"So you like me a lot huh?"

"Yes I do, it's too bad you have to leave. But I don't know how you feel about me?"

"I wish I could stay, Marie Ann, but you know I have to leave. I like you very much, I more than like you. I've never felt like this about a girl before."

"I feel the same way, Patrick."

"Come back to Duncan's apartment with me, Marie Ann. I only have a couple of days before I have to leave. Please?"

They arrived at the apartment. Patrick turned the light on and apologized for the mess. Marie Ann was so nervous her palms were sweating.

"I'm sorry I don't have any wine to offer you, but there are some soft drinks in the fridge."

"Sure, that'll be fine."

They sat on the sofa and drank their sodas in silence. Marie Ann's mind was racing.

She thought. If I sleep with him, what is he going to think of me? I may never see him again. Am I that stupid to believe that he likes me that much? Once he leaves, will I ever hear from him again? It's not too late to tell him that I changed my mind. But if I tell him that, he's going to think I'm just a tease. But if he's the kind of person I think he is, he'll be okay with it.

Suddenly he moved over and put his arm around her, drew her close to him, and kissed her. In that moment, she knew she wasn't going to deny him anything. She kissed him back, their lips tingling with desire.

He stood up and carried her into the bedroom. She said in a soft voice, "Let's not rush, let's make this a special night."

"All right," he responded. It took all the will power he had to comply with her request. Her heart pounded against his. He slowly unbuttoned her dress and watched as it slipped off her body. He stood there for a few moments and gazed upon her beauty. She unbuttoned his shirt and tossed it to the floor.

They fell on the bed in an embrace.

A soft breeze came through the window. He said to her in a soft voice. "Marie Ann, I tell you again, I have never felt like this about another woman before. If I could I would stay with you, but you know the circumstances."

"I know. Just kiss me."

Marie Ann woke up and realized that it was Six a.m. She jumped out of bed and grabbed her clothes.

"What's wrong?" said Patrick.

"It's Six a.m.! she practically shouted. My grandmother has probably called the police by now."

"Why didn't she call you on the cell phone?"

"Because I turned it off before we got here last night. I didn't want anyone to disturb us, and I forgot to turn it back on."

"All right, take it easy, call her and tell her that you're all right. That you'll explain everything when you get home."

"I could try to sneak in, she might still be asleep."

"You don't really believe that, do you?"

"No, not really."

"Do you want me to go with you?"

"No, I'd rather go alone. I'll call you later and let you know what happened."

"All right then, I love you. Believe that, Marie Ann."

"I love you too, Patrick."

Marie Ann parked her car in front of her house. As quickly as she could, she opened the front door and stepped into the hallway. Immediately she spotted her grandmother sitting on the sofa.

"Grandma, please don't be mad at me. I can explain."

"Marie Ann, I realize that you are almost twenty-one, but you could have at least called me."

"Grandma, can I please tell you what happened?"

"All right tell me, but it better be good."

"Well, after we left here, we went to Duncan's apartment to talk. We fell asleep, and by the time we woke up it was six a.m. I got home as soon as I could. That's why I didn't call you."

"I believe the part about you going to Duncan's apartment, but I'm sure you two did more than just talk and sleep. Marie Ann, I wasn't born yesterday. You slept with that boy, didn't you?"

"Yes, Grandma, but I love him."

"Marie Ann, he's leaving for Ireland tomorrow. You may never see him again."

"I know, but I can't help the way I feel. He told me he loves me too."

"You young people now a days fall in love so quickly. Sweetheart, I wish you the best. I hope you get everything you want in life. I want to see you happy before I die."

"Grandma, don't say things like that. I don't know what I would do without you."

Meanwhile, Star couldn't wait to get out of work. She said goodbye to Norma and hurried to catch the shuttle. She planned to go home and write in her diary about how much she missed Rudy. It was Friday; he would probably call her tonight. Lately, she liked to lock herself up in her room and daydream about him.

She would make up scenarios about the two of them getting married. They would have a big wedding on the beach in the spring. It would be a perfect night; the sky would be covered with beautiful stars, and of course there would be a full moon. She would wear a beautiful dress. The dress would be white of course and floor-length, covered with sequence. Rudy would look just as handsome as the prince in her dreams.

There was a knock at the door. She jumped off the bed and unlocked the door. It was Marie Ann.

"Hi. Why are you always locking the door lately? What are you hiding in here?"

"Nothing. I just want some privacy. Inez just comes in as she pleases."

"Why don't you say something to her?"

"She still thinks of me as a little girl. I just don't want to hurt her feelings. So is Patrick still here?"

"Yes, he's leaving tomorrow. Let me tell you what happened."

"What? Tell me?"

"We went over to Duncan's apartment and fell asleep. I didn't get home until after six in the morning. When I got home, my grandmother was furious."

"My dad told me that she called late last night and asked if we had seen you."

"Oh my God, that's so embarrassing."

"So what really happened? Did you sleep with him? And don't lie!"

"Yes."

"What was it like?"

"It was wonderful, Star. I love him, and he told me he loves me too."

"What are you going to do?"

"I don't know. I'll be getting my inheritance pretty soon. I'll have enough money to go to Ireland then. That is, if he really meant what he told me."

"What was that?"

"That he wanted to take me with him. Only I have my grandma to think about. I hate to leave her alone."

"Marie Ann, she was alone before you came into the picture."

On Sunday morning, Stephan told Star that Duncan and Renee were due back from their honeymoon early today.

"I think I'll have them over for dinner tonight so they can tell us all about their trip," he said.

"Where did they go, Dad?"

"They went to some resort in Jamaica."

"Wow, the Caribbean. I'd like to go there some day. Hey Dad, why don't you ask Norma to come to dinner too? After all, she was the maid of honor and she's Renee's best friend."

"All right, I can do that. I'll call her later."

"No, Dad, call her now. What if she makes other plans and can't come."

"All right, all right, I'll call her now."

At dinner Star had many questions about Jamaica. "Was it beautiful?" she asked.

"Yes, it was," said Renee "and we had a wonderful time. We had dinner one night at a restaurant outdoors next to a water-fall and the food was great. We also went horseback riding."

Duncan interrupted. "Only there, they ride English-style, which was the only thing I didn't like. Everything else was great."

"What else?" asked Star.

"We went to a place called Dunn's River Falls." said Renee. "It was wonderful. We got lots of pictures."

"We also went snorkeling," said Duncan, "and I went fishing for sail fish on a boat that wasn't very big. I had loads of fun. We caught two of them."

"That's something I'd like to do some day," said Stephan.

"Sounds like you two had a wonderful honeymoon," said Norma.

"Yes, we did," said Duncan, leaning over and kissing Renee on the cheek.

"Something's missing here, or someone," said Norma. "Where's Marie Ann tonight?"

"She's home brooding," said Star. "Patrick went back to Ireland today."

"Oh, is that so?" said Renee. She looked at Duncan.

"We missed a lot while we were on our honeymoon," said Duncan. "So, Star tell us how all this came about?"

"I don't know if I should say anything, Uncle Duncan. Marie Ann is my best friend. I'll just say that they both liked each other a lot and he had to go back to Ireland, and now she's really sad."

Stephan said, "Okay, now I know why Mrs. Rossi called late the other night looking for Marie Ann. Young love: sometimes you have to get your heart broken several times before the right one comes along."

Star went upstairs after dinner. She couldn't get her dad's words out of her mind. What were the exact words he used?

Sometimes you have to get your heart broken several times before the right ones comes along.

What if Rudy wasn't the right one? Was she going to be crying her eyes out the way poor Marie Ann was now? Patrick hasn't even dumped her yet. What condition would she be in if Rudy were to stop calling her or if he told her he found someone else? What if he wrote her a Dear Jane letter? She knew one thing for sure; she wasn't going to make the same mistake Marie Ann made. She wouldn't sleep with Rudy until she was absolutely sure he loved her.

Her cell phone rang. She knew it was Rudy calling before it even rang.

"Star, I have good news. I'm taking a break for the summer. I'll be coming home the second week in June for almost two months."

"That's great! I can't wait."

After they hung up she thought. *What am I going to tell Rudy? What am I going to tell my dad? Should I say anything at all?* She was sure her dad knew how old Rudy was. If Rudy found out she was barely seventeen, would he still want to see her?

In the morning, at breakfast, Star said to her dad, "Dad, I'm going to be eighteen soon."

"Not until next year, Star."

"Nine months, Dad."

"Ten months. What do you want, Star?"

"Well, I want to start dating boys."

"I'm surprised you haven't done it sooner."

"What?"

"Lots of my colleagues at work have daughters your age, and they tell me they've been dating for a couple of years already. I guess I'm one of the lucky dads who didn't have to worry until now."

"Don't worry about me, Dad. I know what I'm doing."

"I know, Star. I know you're a good girl. I trust you.

But I still want to meet the lucky boys you decide to date, so I can give them the third degree."

"You wouldn't, would you, Dad?"

"Just joking, honey. Don't get so uptight. I'm sure you're not going to bring home some tattooed, earing-wearing guy home."

After her dad left for work she thought, *I wish he hadn't said he trusted me.* She got on the bus and went to school. She didn't start work at Norma's until four in the afternoon. Once Rudy came home, she would try to spend as much time as she could with him. She still had to work at Norma's, but that was just for four hours in the afternoon on Mondays, Wednesdays, and Fridays.

She knew that her dad would eventually find out about Rudy. She had no idea how he would react when he did find out. The only objection he could have was their age difference. But she had heard somewhere that a man should be at least ten years older than a woman. She couldn't remember where she heard that. Maybe it was from Marie Ann.

What was she going to tell Rudy? He was going to want come over to the house to pick her up so that they could go on a date. Her dad would be sure to see him. She had to talk to Marie Ann. *Maybe my problems will get her out of that mood she'd been in since Patrick left.*

Chapter 8

As soon as Star got off work, she boarded the shuttle and went straight home. She had a snack in the kitchen while she talked to Inez.

"How are things going with you, Star?"

"Fine. Why?"

"Because you're either locked up in your room talking on that cell phone, or you're working at that beauty shop. I don't even see Marie Ann around here anymore."

"She works too."

"So you're not going to tell me, huh? What about those boys you were going to start dating?"

"What?" "Yes, Your dad told me."

"Pretty soon, Inez."

"I know something's going on, my little Star, and I'm going to find out what it is."

"There's nothing going on. Boy, you have some imagination. I'm going over to Marie Ann's. Okay, see you later."

Star walked over to Marie Ann's and knocked on the door.

Mrs. Rossi answered.

"Hi, Mrs. Rossi, is Marie Ann here?"

"Yes. She's up in her room. Star, maybe you can get her out of that mood she's been in since that Irish boy left. She just picks at her food; I swear a bird eats more than that girl. I'm worried about her."

"All right, I'll talk to her."

"Thank you, Star."

Star knocked on Marie Ann's bedroom door.

"I'm not hungry, Grandma." Came Marie Ann's voice.

"It's me, Star. Can I come in?"

"Come on in."

Star looked at Marie Ann. She was wearing a night shirt that said. I started out with nothing, and I still have nothing!

"You look terrible," said Star when she saw Marie Ann.

"Thanks."

"You don't go to work looking like that, do you? Have you heard from Patrick?"

"No, I don't go to work looking like this! Yes, and I miss him so much it hurts. Star, I love him so much."

"Marie Ann, your grandma is really worried about you."

"I know she is. I don't mean to worry her, but I can't help it I miss him so much."

"Do you mind if I talk to you about a problem that I have? You're the only one I can talk to about this."

"What is it, Star?"

"Rudy called. He's going to be coming home sooner than I thought."

"When?"

"The second week of June, he'll be here until the first week of September. I told my dad I was going to start dating."

"What did he say?"

"He said it was about time."

"You've got to be kidding."

"That's exactly what he said, but I think he's thinking I'm going to be dating seventeen-or eighteen-year-old boys. Not someone twenty-one years old. I can just hear him. He's not a boy, he's a man."

"Star, I think you should talk to your dad before Rudy comes home."

"It's not as easy as it sounds. I'll think about it. I really like this guy. I think he's the one."

"Be careful, Star. He's had more experiences in life than you have. Don't let him take advantage of you. Don't forget he's your first love. First loves are pretty intense, and you're so young, Star."

"I won't. As much as I care for him, I won't let him talk me into anything I'm not ready for."

"Good. Keep thinking that way."

"How about you and Patrick? How is this long-distance romance working out?"

"I don't know how it's working for him, but I'm a wreck. I miss him so much. In his letters he says he told his parents about me. He wants me to go to Ireland and meet them."

"Are you going?"

"I don't know. I don't even have a passport yet. Not to mention that I haven't said a word to my grandmother about it. You know how I feel about leaving her alone."

"We'll look after her. She has my dad, Inez, and me. Go, Marie Ann, apply for a passport and go."

"What if I go all the way over there for nothing? I want marriage, a home, and eventually children."

"Have you told him that?"

"No."

"Well, tell him. If he wants those things too, then go. I'll miss you, but I'd rather see you happy than looking like this."

"Thanks a lot. Now get out of here, I'm going to write Patrick a letter."

Sunday morning at breakfast Star said to Stephan, "I'm still waiting for those pictures. You promised me you'd find them for me by the weekend. I need them for school, Dad."

"Oh, yes, I did find some of them, but with all that's been going on around here, I forgot to give them to you. I'm playing golf with Duncan this morning. I'll give them to you later."

"Dad, come on. I need them."

"Oh, all right."

He went into his office and opened up one of the desk drawers, took out a folder, and handed it to her.

"Now, was that so hard?" she said.

Just then they heard Duncan honking his car horn.

"Got to go, honey, see you later."

As soon as Stephan left, Star went to her room. She opened up the folder and started looking through the pictures. Most of them were black and white. Some of them were of Stephan as an infant with his mother. Then she came across one of a woman who was holding an infant. The woman looked so much like her. She looked like the woman in her dreams. The woman was wearing a crescent-moon pendant. There was a vase in the background with white flowers.

Who was she? Her dad would know who she was. As soon as he got home, she would ask him.

Star stayed in her room waiting for her dad. Finally, she heard Duncan's car pull into the driveway. She went downstairs as soon as she saw the car drive off.

"Dad," she asked him. "Who is this lady?"

"Why, Star, what's the urgency about knowing who she is?"

"Dad, who is she?"

"It's no secret. She's my grandmother."

"What about the little baby?"

"Oh, that's me."

"Dad, what happened to your mother? You never mention her."

"She died when I was just a year old. She was involved in a terrible car accident. My grandmother raised me after my mother died."

"I'm sorry, Dad."

"It's all right, honey."

"I just wanted to know because of the genealogy class. Your grandmother looks so much like me. Don't you think so, Dad?"

"Yes. She was a very beautiful woman."

"What's that pendant she's wearing?"

"I don't know. She always wore it."

"What kind of flowers are those in that vase?"

"They're white lilacs; they were her favorite flowers."

"Well, thanks for the pictures, Dad."

"No problem."

After Star went up to her room, Stephan worried, wondering whether she had another premonition or another dream. Maybe she had gotten something by touching those pictures, but why didn't she tell him? Well, maybe if she had a boyfriend it would take her mind off her ability.

Very soon he would wish he had never had those thoughts.

While Star was up in her room, she stared at the pictures of her great-grandmother. She wondered if she might be able to get a premonition from them, like when she touched the pearl necklace and the teapot. She put her hands on them and closed her eyes, but nothing happened. Maybe it was just certain objects that gave her the premonitions.

On the Internet, she did some research and found out that some people are born with the gift of premonition, which is a passive gift. Sometimes their premonitions are triggered by touching an object. As time goes by, a person's premonitions get clearer and make more sense to the person having them. It's rare when the person gets the gift of Empathy. Being an Empath allows a person to touch an object and go back to the past to witness what happened at a certain time and place. The power of Empathy is tied to a person's emotions. That person can feel the pain of those he or she sees in her visions.

Like a light bulb going on, she remembered the attic. All these years, ever since she was a child, her dad had tried to keep her out of there. Was it really unsafe? What was he hiding up there?

There had to be a key somewhere in the house. She would wait until her dad went to play golf with Uncle Duncan again.

On Sunday she told Inez she wasn't feeling well and to go to church without her. As soon as Duncan picked her dad up to go and play golf, she started searching the house for the key. She looked everywhere she could think of, but she couldn't find it. It was almost time for Inez to come home from church. She would resume the search another day.

On Monday Star arrived at work.

"Hey Star, how are you?" asked Norma.

"Oh, I'm okay. And you?"

"I'm all right."

"How's your dad?"

"He's okay, working all the time. He never takes time off to relax. You should call him and get together—go to the movies, go to dinner or something, so that he can get out of the house."

"I can't call him."

"Why not? This is the Twenty-first Century."

"I'll think about it."

That evening at dinner Star said, "Dad, you've been working really hard lately. You should take some time off and go have some fun—go to the movies or to dinner."

"When do you want to go?"

"I don't mean with me. Find someone your own age to go with you."

"Now, that really sounds pathetic."

"Oh, Dad, I didn't mean it to. What I mean is that you're always at work or you're stuck in your office here at home. The only time you go out is Sunday mornings to play golf with Uncle Duncan."

"Maybe you're right. I am becoming somewhat of a hermit. There are a couple of paralegals at the firm that are single I could ask one of them out sometime."

Star thought, *Oh, no Norma better call him pretty soon.*

Star went up to her room and called Norma. "Norma, I talked to my dad and he said he felt like he needed to get out and relax. I think he's thinking of asking someone from work out. Why don't you call him?"

"Star, why are you trying to push us together?"

"Well, I figure if my dad's going to take someone out, it might as well be someone I like."

Norma laughed and said, "all right, I'll call him."

Star went back downstairs. She sat in the den and turned on the TV and patiently waited for the phone to ring. After about fifteen minutes, it rang and Stephan answered it.

"Hi, Norma. It's been a while. How are you? Did you want to talk to Star?"

There was silence for a couple of minutes. Then he said, "Sure, why not? I'll pick you up tomorrow about eight."

Star quickly got off the sofa and started walking towards the stairs. Then she heard her dad say. "Just a minute, young lady. Did you arrange that?"

"What?"

"Don't act like you don't know what I'm talking about?"

"All right Dad, I'm guilty. But, Dad, go out with Norma just this one time. If you don't have fun with her, you don't have to call her again. You can always blame it all on me."

"I have no choice. I couldn't very well say no. Star, promise me you won't pull another stunt like this again?"

"All right, Dad. I promise."

"Good night, honey."

"Good night, Dad."

Saturday evening, Stephan was getting ready to go and pick up Norma to take her to the movies.

"What movie are you going to see, Dad?"

"I don't know. I'll leave it up to Norma. She'll probably choose a love story."

"You don't know that, Dad. You've already made up your mind that you're not going to have a good time, haven't you?"

"No, but I know women."

"How can you know women? You've been stuck in the house for seventeen years with me and Inez."

"Okay smarty pants, like I said, I know women."

"Oh, you're impossible, Dad. Please try to have a good time for Norma's sake." She crossed her fingers as he went out the front door.

Inez came out of the kitchen, "I can't believe that your dad had a date," she said.

Star looked at her, and said. "Neither can I."

She went back to the den to watch TV until Inez decided to go to bed. She waited about twenty minutes. Then she went into her dad's office to look for the key to the attic. She had to be careful to put everything back exactly the way she found it. The key wasn't anywhere in his office. She decided to go upstairs and look in his bedroom. But the key wasn't there either; he must have it on him. Darn. How was she supposed to get that key now?

The next morning at breakfast, she asked her dad, "How was your date with Norma?"

"I shouldn't tell you anything, the way you tricked us."

"Dad, come on, tell me."

"All right, but only because you're still my little Star."

"Oh, Dad, I told you, I'm all grown up."

"Never."

"Come on, Dad, spill it."

"Well, I actually had a good time with Norma. First off, I thought she was going to choose *My Big Fat Greek Wedding*. Instead she chose the one I wanted to see, *Adaptation*."

"See, Dad, I told you. Then what happened?"

"After the movie, I took her for a late supper at a nice restaurant."

"Were there candles and flowers on the table?"

"Star, this was our first date or, should I say, trick date."

"Did you kiss her goodnight?"

"All right, Star, that's going a little bit too far."

"That means you did."

Just then Duncan, was outside, honking his car horn.

"I have to run. See you later, honey."

"Bye, Dad."

Well, she thought, that *worked out well. Now about that key?*

How am I going to get into that attic?

Inez came out of the kitchen. "Star, I'm going to the ten o'clock Mass. Are you coming with me?"

"Yeah, I just have to go upstairs and finish getting ready. I'll just be a few minutes."

After Mass was over, Star asked Inez, "Inez, you haven't visited your cousin Lupe for a while. How come?"

"Oh, I don't know. She's into something called bunko with some of the other house keepers. Last time we talked she got mad at me because I told her I didn't have time for dumb games. That it was just an excuse to get together and gossip."

"Inez, she's the only family you have here."

"I know, but she got me mad."

"Why don't you call her and make up? The two of you can go and watch one of those Mexican movies you like so much."

"Maybe. I'll think about it. Oh, you're getting too smart for your britches, *meja*."

On Monday, Star arrived at Norma's salon early.

"Hi, Norma. How was your date with my dad?"

"We had a nice time."

"That's all?"

"I'm sure you already gave your dad the third degree."

"Yeah, but he was no help."

Norma laughed. "Well, all I'm going to tell you is that I really had a good time. And yes, he kissed me goodnight. Now get to work."

"Okay. That's all I wanted to know."

Chapter 9

Weeks passed, and Star was no closer to figuring out how she was going to get inside that attic. She had to talk to someone she could trust. It was Tuesday, and Marie Ann would be home for sure.

Marie Ann was lying in bed thinking about Patrick when the phone rang.

"It's me, Star. Can you come over? I really need you."

"I'm not feeling good."

"Please, Marie Ann, I need you to come over and bring your tarot cards."

"All right. I'll be over in a little while."

When Marie Ann got there, Star said to her. "You look like death warmed over."

"Where did you hear that?"

"I don't know, but never mind. Let's go up to my room. Did you bring the cards?"

"Yes. What's going on, Star?"

"Wait until we go up to my room."

Once they were in Star's bedroom. Marie Ann demanded to know what was going on.

"First I want to ask you something. Did you talk to Patrick about the way you feel about him and what you want?"

"No, not yet."

"What are you waiting for?"

"I'm afraid of what he might say. I'm afraid he might not want what I want."

"You're never going to find out unless you ask him."

"All right, I guess I might as well ask him and get it over with."

"You promise?"

"I Promise. But first I want to go to L.A. to get my cards read. I used to go there when I was living with my aunt. I know you probably don't believe in that, but I do."

"You'd be surprised what I believe in."

"What do you mean?"

"Don't get mad at me because I haven't told you this before. It wasn't that I didn't trust you. It's just that I've had trouble dealing with it all my life. My dad is the only one who knows about it."

"Knows about what?"

"All right. Ever since I was a little kid I've had premonitions."

"What kind of premonitions?"

"Well, at first I just knew when the phone was about to ring before it rang. I knew that someone was coming to the house before my dad or Inez did. If something bad happened in the neighborhood like an accident or someone died, I knew before anyone else. I had a lot of problems with the kids in school because of it. They made fun of me and called me witch. As I got older they just gave me these weird looks."

"Oh, Star, I'm so sorry."

"Didn't you ever wonder why you were my only friend?"

"Well sort of, but I thought you were just shy."

"Anyway, now that I'm older, my gifts seem to have grown with me."

"What do you mean?"

"Remember the first time we went to see you at the antique shop?"

"Yes, you were with Renee and Norma."

"That was the first time I was able to touch an object and go back to the past. There was a pearl necklace on the counter. It was really pretty. When I went to pick it up, as soon as I put my hands on it I couldn't help closing my eyes. All of a sudden I saw a lovely woman wearing the necklace. I could hear orchestra music in the background, and she was wearing an old-fashioned ball gown. It's only happened a couple of times and only with old objects.

"I got on the internet and found out that some people who have premonitions become Empaths; it's an inherited gift. Also, as their power grows they can develop what is known as precognition. It means to be able to see into the future."

"So what you're telling me is that all your life you've had premonitions, and now you can touch certain objects and regress back to the past? Also that later on you may be able to see the future?"

"I don't know that for sure. It hasn't happened yet."

"Wow, when you called and asked me to come over, this was the last thing I thought you were going to tell me."

"Do you believe everything I've told you?"

"Star, I've known you long enough to know that you wouldn't lie to me about something like this."

"Can we keep it between the two of us? Don't even tell Patrick?"

"Don't worry, your secret is safe with me. Besides, who would believe me?"

"The reason I called was I wanted to tell you what I just told you, and I want you to read my cards."

"Really, I wondered why you asked me to bring them."

They sat on the floor.

"All right, Star, shuffle the cards and then hand them to me." Marie Ann did the spread.

Marie Ann said, "The first card represents the present. It's the beaming light."

"What does it mean?"

"It means a happy union, friendship, a good friend, good health. The second card is immediate influence—Star of the Magicians. It means joy, trust, and optimism. The third card is goal or destiny, an important card. The fourth card is the wheel of fortune; a matter is brought to a successful end. The fifth card is the distant past, the veiled lamp. The hermit: unselfish kept secrets, loneliness, silence, and patience. The sixth card—you can ask a question."

"Gosh, I have two questions. I don't know which one to ask."

"Only one, Star."

"Will I be able to open the attic door soon?"

Marie Ann looked at Star, puzzled.

"I'll explain later."

"All right. The card says you will fulfill your task. The seventh card is the balance of swords. Justice, good relation-ships with people, open-minded and truthful. The eighth card is the two paths. Arrive at a decision; the right choice will result in harmony and success. The last card is the final result. The reading looks good. Make sure you make the right choice where Rudy is concerned. You know what I mean?"

"I know what you mean. Thanks. That was a good reading."

"So, what's this about an attic?"

"Ever since I was a little kid, my dad tried to keep me out of our house's attic. He keeps it locked; Inez can't even go in there. I've searched the whole house for the key, but I can't find it. I think he has it with him all the time."

"Are you serious?"

"I've got to get into that attic. I just know there's something in there he doesn't want me to see."

"Why don't you just ask him? All he can say is no."

"You know what? You're right. I'm going to do just that as soon as he gets home tonight."

"Good. I'd better go now."

"I'll go with you to L.A. when you're ready to go and get your cards read."

"You will! Thanks, Star. How about this weekend?"

"Sure, it's not like I have anything else to do."

"All right, see you then."

When Stephan came home from work, Star waited until they finished dinner. Then she said, "Dad I want you to open the attic door. I want to see what's in there?"

"What? Where did this come from?"

"Dad, for a long time I've known there was something up there you don't want me to see."

"Star, I told you before, it's not safe up there."

"I'm sorry, Dad, I don't believe you."

"So you think I'm lying to you?"

"Please, Dad, tell me the truth. What's in the attic? Listen, I already know all about myself. I went on the Internet and found out about my premonitions. I found out that they're inherited and that I have developed the gift of Empathy. Dad, I know my gift is growing and that I could develop what is called precognition, which means I would be able to see the future. The only thing I don't know Dad, is, why me?"

"Come here, honey," he said. He hugged her. "Star, I was going to wait until you turned eighteen."

"Wait for what, Dad? You're scaring me."

"Come on, honey. I'll take you up to the attic."

Stephan unlocked the attic door. They walked in slowly while he looked for the light switch. Star stood and looked around. There was an old chandelier hanging from the ceiling and an old wooden table with two unpainted chairs. The chairs looked like they might have been painted blue at one time. Two oriental rugs lay on the floor, an old crocheted blanket was thrown over an old-fashioned rocker and an old footstool stood against the wall. The room was filled with antique furniture, a layer of cobwebs, hung from the ceiling and clung to the furniture and walls.

Then she spotted an old trunk, she walked towards it. Stephan stopped her.

"Before you open the trunk, honey, I want to explain something to you. Come over here and sit down."

Stephan began by explaining to Star about her heritage.

"My great-grandparents were born in Romania. They came to this country many years ago. They were Shuvani Gypsies."

"What's a Shuvani?"

"The word Shuvani is the same as the word *witch*."

"Dad are you telling me that your great-grandmother was a witch?"

"Star, will you let me finish?"

"All right. Go on, Dad."

"In the old days, *witch* meant *wise* one to the people like the gypsies. The wise one was able to cure disease with herbs and stones and cast magical spells. Witches were never considered evil in those days. They were just people with powers. They helped the people in their tribes. The Shuvani gypsy was usually the head of the tribe and very respected for their knowledge of magic and healing. Most Shuvanis were women, but there were some men.

"Gypsies have been accused of dealing in black magic, even making deals with the devil and other terrible things. Gypsies have been persecuted as recently as the twentieth century. My grandmother told me her secret just before she died. She also told me that if I were to get married and produce a girl-child, and if that girl-child was born during the Spring Equinox, that she would be very special.

"I was as much in the dark as you are, Star. Anyway, she told me that only girl-children in our family possess certain powers, powers like the ones you have. Others can read minds, some are healers and there have been many with other powers. Of course you can reject your gift if you want, try to ignore it, and hope eventually it goes away. I don't know if that will work. I didn't have time to discuss that with my grandmother before she died. I know this is a lot for you to think about."

Star silently stepped over to the trunk and opened it. The first thing she saw was a small walnut chest. A gold candelabra and three white candles lay in the corner of the trunk. A colorful shawl was thrown over something; she reached in and grabbed the shawl and saw a large book. She picked it up and walked over to the table and put it down.

The book had a large insignia of a crescent-moon with a moonstone embossed in the center of it.

"Dad, I've been dreaming about a crescent-moon pendant that looks just like this."

"My grandmother wore a pendant that looked just like that. It was passed down from Shuvani mother to daughter in our family. It's a crescent moon with a moonstone. It stands for female wisdom and energy; it helps to strengthen intuition and psychic perception. They also believe it has the power to grant wishes to the Shuvani who wears it. They say it helps you to see things more clearly."

Star opened the book to the first page. "Look, Dad, it's a small picture frame. It looks like a Saint. There's some words written on it." She picked it up. "It's in a foreign language."

"It's Latin. The Saint is St. Cipriano, Saint of the Magicians or of anyone who cast spells to heal. He is known for three things. He is the Patron Saint of the Magicians, author of the famous "Grimoire," or book of magic, and last he provides protection against powerful demons, spells, and other dark magic."

She turned to the second page. There was a sheet of paper, written in English. It explained that every page would be translated in English. "It's a book of spells."

"Not just spells, Star. There are healing recipes in there, rhymes on how to ward off evil. There are also a couple of pages on how gypsy weddings are performed. There's another page in there on welcoming a new baby. They also put instructions on how to prepare for a parent's death. There's a section in there that might interest you on how to make amulets, talismans, and healing pouches. Almost anything you want to know is in that book."

"It's going to take me a long time to read it."

"I'm going to ask you one favor, Star. Don't take the book out of the attic or out of this house, please. I'll give you a key; in fact, I'll have a copy made in case one of them gets lost."

"Okay, Dad, I promise. I want to see what's in that little chest."

She walked back to the trunk and reached in and picked up the small chest. She put it on the table and opened it. Inside were two white pillar candles, a silver knife with a carved handle, and an incense burner.

"What are these, Dad?"

"Those are quarts clusters."

"What are they for?"

"I don't know. You'll have to look it up in the book."

She reached inside and picked up a pendant that was lying on a green pouch.

"Dad, is this your grandmother's pendant?"

"Yes, but it's yours now."

"It's beautiful, Dad. Can I really keep it?"

"Yes, but it's our secret, remember? Star, be careful where you wear that pendant."

"What do you mean, Dad?"

"I know it's the twentieth-first century, but there are some people out there who are still living in the past."

"Like who, Dad?"

"I don't want to mention any names, but some people will call you a witch just because you're wearing a crystal. If you want to wear it, that's fine but try not to display it too much."

"All right, Dad. Dad I have something to tell you."

"What is it, Star?"

"I already told Marie Ann."

"What did you tell her?"

"I told her about my premonitions; I told her about the attic."

"What do you mean you told her about the attic?"

"Well, I was going to try to get in here by myself. I thought you were hiding something from me. I looked for the key, but I couldn't find it. So I told Marie Ann and she said I should talk to you about it."

"I guess it's my fault. I should have told you about it sooner."

"Dad, she promised she wouldn't say anything to anyone."

"Come on, Star, let's put these things away for now. It's getting late."

Star walked over to the trunk with the little chest.

"What are those colorful stones scattered inside the trunk?" she asked.

"They used stones and herbs for healing and spell works," said her dad.

"Dad, what did they need a knife for?"

"The knife was used to cut herbs from their gardens that they later used for healing. You'll have to read the book to find out whatever else you want to know."

They put everything away, closed the trunk, and locked the attic door.

Chapter 10

Star felt like she had to tell Marie Ann what she had found in the attic. She would never forgive herself if she didn't tell her. She would make her swear to keep it to herself.

"I got into the attic." She told Marie Ann on the phone. "We'll get together soon and I'll tell you everything, okay?"

"All right, but soon, Star."

A few days had passed since Star and her dad went up to the attic. At dinner Stephan asked Star? If she had been getting enough sleep lately.

"Sure I have, Dad. Why do you ask?"

"Because you're starting to get black circles under your eyes. That's a sure sign of lack of sleep. Star, I know what's going on. Your pulled between school, work, and waiting until Inez goes to sleep so that you can sneak up to the attic and read that darn book. This has to stop. I wish I had gotten rid of that darn thing. It's going to start affecting your health."

"Okay, Dad, you're right. I'll only go up there on weekends."

"All right, but I'll be watching you."

Her dad was right. Not only was she busy with school and work and reading the book, but she was always thinking about Rudy and anxiously waiting for him to call. When he did, she stayed on the phone with him as long as she could.

She looked at herself in the mirror. Her dad was right. She was starting to get circles under her eyes. They weren't as bad as he said; he was exaggerating, of course. With a little make-up, they would disappear. Tomorrow she would go and see what Marie Ann was doing.

The next morning, after she had breakfast with Inez, she walked over to visit Marie Ann. When she got there she asked Marie Ann. "So, how are things?"

"A little better. I applied for my passport."

"Great. Did you tell your grandmother?"

"No, not yet."

"What are you waiting for?"

"I don't know. I guess I'm afraid of what she's going to say."

"Like what?"

"Like, are you crazy, you just met this boy and you want to go running off all the way to Ireland."

"She wouldn't say that."

"She might, or even worse, she might say I'm going to go and leave her all alone."

"I can't believe she'd say that either. What does Patrick say?"

"He wants me to come to Ireland as soon as possible. He says he misses me like crazy."

"But enough about me," Marie Ann went on. "Now tell me what you found in the attic?"

"Well, there was this big old trunk and inside there was this big book and some other stuff. It was a book of spells, rituals and cures and all kinds of things."

"Was it a book of shadows?"

"What's a book of shadows?"

"The wiccans keep a book of shadows where they record all their spells and other things; it's like a magical diary."

"How do you know all this?"

"The internet that's how."

"What else was in there?"

"There was a small chest with same candles, a knife and some stones. Oh, and a pendant it belonged to my ancestors, all women. You're not going to believe this they were gypsy women from Romania."

"Really, you hit the jackpot."

"Not really. What is Rudy going to say if he ever finds out?"

"Don't worry about Rudy, Star. There will probably be a lot more boys in your life besides Rudy. You're still so young there'll be other guys."

"I want Rudy—I don't want anyone else!"

"Boy, you're really into him, aren't you? Like I said, be careful with him. I told you before, first loves can be killers. They can end up almost killing your soul."

"Don't exaggerate. He's not that way."

"That's what I thought about Julian and look what happened to me."

"Let's stop talking about this. Do you still want to go to L.A to get your cards read?"

"Yes, let's go tomorrow early in the morning."

"Okay, Inez can go to church without me. I'll come over about eight o'clock. Is that okay?"

"Sure, that's okay. After we get back I'll talk to my grandmother."

"You promise?"

"I promise"

The next day, Star told Stephan they were going shopping and that they probably wouldn't be back until the afternoon. She didn't want him to know they were driving all the way into L.A. He worried too much about her. They left early and headed for L.A.

"Where is this place?" asked Star. As they drove around the strange, neighborhood in L.A.?

"She works out of a place called The Elements. We're almost there. Don't worry. You can go in with me or you can stay and look around the shop while I get my cards read—Oh, look, there it is. Now let's see if I can find a place to park."

They walked into the shop. Star had never seen a place like this before. Marie Ann walked up to the counter and talked to a woman there. "I called yesterday and made an appointment with Madam Mariska. I'm a little early.

"Come on, Star, let's look around while we wait."

Star was amazed at what she saw. There were books on the occult, and on how to be a solitary witch, spirit guides, angel guides, and Wicca. She saw crystals of all colors, and sizes, and shapes; jewelry, and tarot cards. As she walked through the aisles, she saw candles of all colors and sizes sitting on the shelves and bowls of colorful stones like the ones in the trunk at home.

"Are you coming with me or are you staying here?" asked Marie Ann.

"I'll go with you."

They walked to the back of the shop; two curtains hung in the doorway. Behind the curtains sat a woman at a round table. She looked like she was in her late fifties. She wore a simple red dress, big hoop earrings, rings on every finger, and many bracelets.

She greeted Marie Ann. "It's been a long time, since you've come to visit."

"Yes it has. I moved to Agoura with my grandmother. This is my friend Star. Star, this is Madam Mariska. Is it all right if she just sits here and observes?"

"That will be fine. Take a seat over there." Madam Mariska pointed towards an ottoman near the table.

"So, my dear, will it be the cards as always, or should I read your palm this time or maybe the tea leaves?"

"I think I'll do something different this time and have you do the tea leaves."

"All right," said Madam Mariska. She got up and put the teapot on a two-burner stove. She went to a small cupboard and got out a plain cup and saucer. Then she got a box of what looked like Chinese tea and put some in the cup. When the pot whistled, she took it off the burner and poured the hot water into the cup.

She placed the cup in front of Marie Ann. She told her to drink it as soon as it cooled down, and to leave about a teaspoon of liquid on the bottom of the cup. Once she had drank most of the tea, Madam Mariska told her to take the cup by the handle and rotate it three times counter-clockwise. Then she said, "Try to swirl the liquid around the cup, spreading the leaves around the bottom and the sides and up towards the rim." Madam Mariska put a napkin on the saucer and told Marie Ann to tip the cup upside down on top of the saucer.

Then Madam Mariska said. "All right, Marie Ann, make a wish."

Marie Ann closed her eyes and made her wish.

Madam Mariska looked at the cup and said, "The airplane—a possible journey or wedding or both."

By the time they left the Elements, Marie Ann was all smiles.

"So are you going to talk to your grandmother now?" asked Star.

"Yes, as soon as I get home, before I lose my nerve"

"Don't forget to call me and let me know what happened."

Marie Ann parked her car in front of her house. Star wished her luck and walked home.

The next day, as soon as Star got home from work, she called Marie Ann. "Well did you talk to your grandmother?"

"Yes. I'll come over and talk to you after dinner."

"Okay, but try to get here as soon as you can."

After dinner Star and Marie Ann went upstairs to Star's bedroom to talk.

"Well," asked Star. "Tell me all about it and don't leave anything out!"

"I'm going to Ireland."

"Really? Tell me everything!"

"Well, as soon as I got home I talked to my grandmother. I told her that we were in love and that Patrick wanted me to go to Ireland to be with him. I told her that his parents knew about me and that they were anxious to meet me. She said that it was up to me if I wanted to go, that it was my life. The best part was that she let me call Patrick to let him know I was going. You're not going to believe this."

"What? Just tell me!"

"As soon as I get there we're getting married. His mother is making all the arrangements. It's going to be a small wedding for family and some family friends. I told my grandmother to apply for a passport, and as soon as she gets it I want her to go to Ireland and visit us."

"I don't know what to say. I hate to lose you. You know that you're my only friend. Of course I'm happy for you."

"Don't be sad, Star, you have Rudy now."

"Yes, but you're the only one who knows my secret besides Dad."

They went downstairs and told Stephan and Inez the good news.

"Well," said Stephan. "This is some surprise. I had no idea. You will be missed around here; you've been like a part of this family. I know Star will miss you the most, other than your grandmother. How does your grandmother feel about all this?"

"She was very understanding and she said she would miss me. As soon as she gets her passport, I want her to go to Ireland to meet Patrick's family."

"Well, that's just great. You know we'll all look after her for you, Marie Ann."

"Thank you, Stephan, thank you so much, thank you, all of you."

"We're going to want to see pictures of the wedding," said Stephan.

"Sure, I'll send lots."

"When are you leaving?" asked Inez.

"I'm not sure. I have to call the airport and make reservations tonight. I'll let you know as soon as I find out." After Marie Ann left, Star sat on the sofa and stared at the TV.

"Honey," said Stephan, "I know you're going to be lonely without her. You know you're going to be graduating in June. You haven't said anything about what college you want to attend or what you want to do with your life once you graduate."

Star thought to herself, *I'd like to marry Rudy and live happily ever after.*

"That's because I don't know, Dad," she said. "I've got this secret life that no one knows about except you and my best friend. And now she's leaving the country to go and marry the man she loves. She was the only friend I had in the world. What am I supposed to do now?"

"I don't know, honey. I wish I had a solution for your problem, but I don't. Didn't you tell me you were going to start dating soon? What happened to that plan?"

"I have to get asked out first, Dad."

"Those boys in your school must be blind."

"Well I have been asked out, but only by nerds and losers."

"Maybe you're just too picky, Star."

"No, Dad, believe me, I'm not."

"One of these days the right guy will come along, and then it will be love at first sight."

"If you ask me, you've been reading too many romance magazines."

"But how about you, Dad? You said you had a good time with Norma on your date?"

"It was all right."

"What happened? What did you do?"

"I didn't do anything. I just haven't called her. I've been really busy."

"Dad you're always busy. What's the real reason? Don't you like her?"

"Sure, I like her. She's a real nice lady."

"Dad, you talk about her as if she were ready to collect social security. You know, Norma's a lot younger than you are. Let's see, I think Renee said she was only about twenty-nine."

"All right, Star. Let's table this conversation for another day. I still have a lot of work for tomorrow."

After Star went upstairs, Stephan thought about what she had said to him. He actually did like Norma; she was a lot of fun to be with and not bad to look at either. He had a good time with her when he took her out. He picked up the phone and called her.

"Hello, Norma, this is Stephan."

"Oh hi, Stephan. I knew it was you."

"You did how?"

"I recognized your voice."

"Oh. The reason I called, I was wondering if you would like to have dinner with me again? I really had a good time the last time we went out. I haven't called you sooner because I've been really busy at the office."

"Stephan, you don't have to explain anything to me. I'd be happy to have dinner with you again."

After he hung up the phone he didn't realize that he was grinning from ear to ear. After that it became a routine. Stephan was dating Norma; they were an item. That made Star very happy; he would be too busy with Norma when Rudy came home. Maybe her dad wouldn't see Rudy and they could avoid all the unpleasantness of an argument about how he was too old for her.

Marie Ann was leaving for Ireland in a few days. Star asked Inez to make a special dinner for her. On Saturday everyone gathered at Star's house for the good-bye dinner.

At the dinner table Stephan stood up and made a toast.

"Here's to Marie Ann and Patrick. May they have a long and happy life in Ireland."

Star stood up with tears in her eyes. "I'm going to miss you so much. You've been my best friend and you've been like the sister I never had. I wish you all the luck in the world."

Duncan stood up and said, "Renee and I want to welcome you to the family. Patrick chose well. They're going to love you over there just like we all do here."

Marie Ann stood up with tears in her eyes and said, "I'm going to miss all of you, most of all you, grandma. I love you so much, and you, Star, I'll never forget all the times we spent together. When you fall in love, I hope it's with someone as special as Patrick."

Before Marie Ann and her grandmother left that night, Stephan said. "Don't forget to write. Let us know if you see any leprechauns."

Marie Ann laughed. "Oh Stephan I won't. You're still taking me to the airport, aren't you?"

"Don't worry, Star and I will be there to pick you up and get you to the airport on time."

On the way back from saying good-bye to Marie Ann at the airport, all Star could think about was Rudy. He would be home soon. Should she tell her dad the truth, or should she sneak around until she got caught and face the consequences?

"What's wrong?" asked Stephan.

"Nothing. I'm just thinking about Marie Ann and how much I'm going to miss her."

"Well, I agree with you, things are certainly going to be different around here without her."

Indeed, Stephan had no idea how different things were going to be very soon.

*C*hapter 11

*T*hat night Star went up to the attic, where she enjoyed reading the book. She was especially interested in the passages that told how to heal with herbs and stones. She was also interested in some of the spells. It said whatever spells they cast were spells for good, never for evil. Unless it was to cast out evil.

She put the book away and walked over to the bookshelf that stood against the wall. It had never occurred to her that there might be books of importance there. She looked though them and found some on magical herbs and roots and another one on flower magic. She kept looking and found one that gave the phases of the moon, one on candle magic, and another one on crystals—their uses and meanings.

All these books were handwritten, and translated. Just like the big book she had found in the trunk, and they were all unsigned. She was overwhelmed. She didn't know which book to read first. She decided that the big book she found in the trunk would be the first one she would finish reading. From what she had already read, she knew she could learn a lot from it. After that, she would read the rest of them one by one.

One evening after Stephan had gone to pick up Norma for a date, Star was up in her bedroom. The doorbell rang and Inez answered the door.

"Hello, my name is Rudy Linarez," said the young man who had rang the bell. He shook her hand, and said. "I'm here to see Star, you must be Inez, is she here?"

"Yes she is and yes I'm Inez, come in." She led him to the den and asked him to wait.

Inez went upstairs and knocked on Star's door. She said, "I told you I knew something was going on, and I told you I would find out what it was."

"What's the matter, Inez?"

"Well, there's a young man downstairs. He says he's here to see you. He says his name is Rudy Linarez."

Star was struck speechless for a few seconds. "He's here now—downstairs?"

"That's what I just said. He's sitting in the den as we speak."

"Oh my God!"

"Star, what's going on?"

"Inez you have to help me. My dad doesn't know anything about him yet. Please, tomorrow I'll tell you everything, please don't tell my dad."

"All right, but tomorrow I want to hear all about it. And only because I like the boy."

"Thank you, Inez. Tell him I'll be right down."

Star ran and looked at herself in the mirror. She combed her hair and put on some lip gloss and a fresh blouse. She ran part of the way down the stairs and walked the rest of the way. As soon as she saw him, she asked him, "What are you doing here?"

"I came to surprise you."

"You sure did. Why don't we go for a ride? Let me tell Inez. I'll be back later Inez we're going for a ride, remember what we talked about."

When she was in the car with Rudy, she decided to come clean with him. "Rudy can we go somewhere private? There's something I want to talk to you about."

"Sure. There's a nice café near the beach on Kanan Road."

When they got there, Rudy ordered appetizers.

"So what did you want to talk to me about?"

"Actually, there are several things I want to talk to you about. First, I want to ask you how you really feel about me, and Rudy, it's important to me."

"Well, Star, the first time I laid eyes on you I knew you were the one for me."

"You mean it?"

"Yes, Star I really mean it!"

"Rudy, it's important to me, to know how you really feel about me."

"You're going to make me say it, aren't you? Well, Star, if you really want to know? I wake up thinking about you. I think about you when I'm studying, I think about you when I'm out in the field working. I think about you before I go to sleep. I seem to always be thinking about you. I just can't seem to stop thinking about you. It's like you've bewitched me."

"Don't say that. Even if I could bewitch you, I wouldn't."

"I'm just joking, Star. So, you said you had several things you wanted to talk to me about?"

"Please don't get mad at me, but I lied to you."

"You lied to me about what?"

"When I told you I was almost eighteen."

"How old are you?"

"I will be eighteen, but not until next June."

"Star, what does your father say about this?"

"He doesn't know about you. Please, Rudy, don't be mad, I didn't tell you the truth because I was afraid to lose you."

"Star, you'll never lose me. I love you. I don't care how young or old you are."

"I love you too, Rudy."

They looked into each other's eyes and kissed across the table.

"Was that all you wanted to tell me?"

"No, after I tell you this, you may not love me after all." "That's not possible."

"Well, here goes. My ancestors are Romanians."

"Oh. I didn't know that."

"Only, the women in our family have special abilities."

"What do you mean, special abilities?"

"Some of them have been healers, some of them could see the future, and some of them could read minds, and other things. I just found out about it not too long ago. No one knows about this except my dad and my friend Marie Ann."

"What about you, Star, do you have any special abilities?"

Star took out her pendant and said. "Yes. I have premonitions and I've recently become an Empath. This pendant belonged to my great-grandmother and to her ancestors before her. It's a crescent moon with a moonstone. The moonstone is a women's stone, a stone of wishes and intuition. It soothes and balances the emotions."

Rudy was silent.

"Well?" said Star. "Please say something."

"Star, right now you're probably thinking that I'm going to drive you home and that you'll never see me again."

"Something like that."

"I'm going to tell you a little story. My grandfather lives in a remote village in Yucatan, Mexico. The last time I heard, there were about five hundred people living in that village. My grandfather is what they call in Mexico a *Curandero*. They also have these people here in the US. *Curandero* means *healer*. Those people are very respected by those who believe in them.

"My grandfather uses non-traditional methods of healing. The treatments can consist of potions, herbs, or magic, depending on what the illness is. He never takes money for his services. He does, however, accept food or an animal now and then or whatever he may need at the time. No one knows about what I just told you. My father's ashamed of what my grandfather is and does."

"Why is he ashamed?"

"Star, I'm surprised my father didn't change his name to Lewis or Lawson or something like that. He's ashamed of who he is. I think he married my mother just so that he could fit in with his associates."

"What nationality is your mother?"

"She's half-German and half-English."

"That's where you get your green eyes from."

"Star, what you told me isn't going to send me to the nearest Catholic Church to acquire some holy water so that I can squirt you with it the next time I see you. I know more about what you just told me than you think." He smiled at her.

"We have one major problem: my dad. When he finds out I'm dating someone four years older than I am he's going to have a cow."

"Do you really think he's going to get that upset?"

"The first boy I bring home for him to meet is a college student who is four years older than I am, and Raymond Linarez's son. What do you think?"

"You have a point. What should we do?"

"I thought of sneaking around, but that's not going to work. Eventually he would find out. I think we should just confront my dad and let him have his fit. He'll get over it eventually and then everything will be all right."

"You think?"

"I hope so. Let me talk to Inez tonight first, and then I'll call you tomorrow and then decide what to do about my dad."

Rudy drove her home. She wouldn't let him walk her to the door in case her dad might be home from his date with Norma. He kissed her goodnight and drove off.

When she walked into the house, Stephan wasn't home from his date with Norma. Inez was in the den watching TV. When she heard Star come in, she turned off the TV. She caught Star before she went upstairs. "Okay, Star. Tell me all about it!"

Star told Inez the whole story about how she met Rudy and that they were in love.

Inez said, "Talk to your dad, Star. He's a reasonable man. At first he won't like it, but after he thinks about it he'll come around. You'll see."

"I hope so, Inez. No matter what he says, I'm not giving him up. I love him."

Inez just looked at her, shook her head, and walked away.

The next day, Star called Rudy. "Can you come over to my house about eight o'clock tonight? I want my dad to meet you."

"Are you sure Star?"

"Yes, let's just get it over with."

"All right. See you then."

That night after dinner, Star told Stephan she wanted to talk to him about something important. They sat in the den. Inez stood nearby, listening to everything.

"Dad, I have a boyfriend."

"You do! When did this happen?"

"The night of Uncle Duncan and Renee's wedding reception."

"Why haven't you said anything until now?"

"He's been away at school in San Francisco. We've been talking on the phone since that day. He's back now. I invited him to come and meet you tonight."

"What's this boy's name?"

"His name is Rudy."

Just then the doorbell rang. "That must be him." She stood up and went to the door.

Stephan was in shock. He knew this day was coming, but did it have to be so soon? Who was this mysterious boy that she had kept hidden from him until now?

Star and Rudy walked into the den. Stephan stood up to greet him and immediately asked, "Don't I know you?"

"I think you know my father, Raymond Linarez."

All of a sudden, Stephan's face turned beet-red. "Aren't you in college? he asked Rudy.

"Yes, I am, sir."

"How old are you, Rudy?"

"I'm twenty-one."

"Do you know that Star is only seventeen?"

"Yes, I found out last night."

"Dad, he thought I was eighteen hum! I lied to him."

"I can't let my seventeen-year-old daughter go out with a twenty-one-year-old man."

"Dad, I love Rudy and he loves me. Please don't try to stop us from seeing each other. If you do, as soon as I turn eighteen you won't be able to keep us apart. Oh, and Rudy knows all about me."

"What do you mean, he knows all about you?"

"You know what I'm talking about. Our secret that only you and Marie Ann know."

"I think you're making a big mistake, Star. I have to think about this." He walked passed them without saying a word and went upstairs.

Inez walked in and said, "That went better than I thought it would."

"Inez, you know Rudy, don't you?"

"Yes, I met him already"

"Did you hear what we were saying?"

"Every word."

"Why do you ask?"

"No reason."

"Star, I have taken care of you since you were a few days old. Do you think I don't know everything that goes on in this house? I know all about your premonitions. I've known since the first time you came running to tell me when you were just a little girl that Mr. Johnson was going to die. Then about a week later he died and again, you told me the neighbor was going to have an accident and a few days later she did. The list went on and on. Don't worry about your dad. He'll calm down."

"Inez, I had no idea you knew. Why didn't you tell me or my dad."

"I figured if you wanted me to know, you would have told me or your dad would have told me. As for you, young man, I would leave before Stephan changes his mind and comes back downstairs tonight."

"She's right, Rudy. Maybe you'd better go. I'll walk you to the door. I'll call you tomorrow and let you know what else he has to say."

They kissed goodnight. Even though her dad was upset, she was glad it was finally over with. At least part one was. Tomorrow she would see what part two would bring.

At breakfast Stephan told Star, "I don't want to talk about it right now. I've still got a lot to think about before I decide what to do."

"How long is it going to take, Dad?"

"As long as it takes. I've got to go to work now."

"All right, Dad." She stood up and kissed him on the cheek.

Inez came out of the kitchen and said, "If that doesn't change his mind nothing will." Star just looked at her and sighed.

She went to work and told Norma all about Rudy and what had happened with her dad. She said, "Norma, maybe you could talk to my dad. He might listen to you."

"Star, I won't bring up the subject, but if he does I'll definitely put in my two cents."

"What are your two cents?"

"That a girl or woman at seventeen or eighteen knows her own heart. Right or wrong, if he stops you from going out with Rudy, you may never forgive him."

"You're right. I never would."

A week went by and Star barely spoke to her dad. But on Saturday Stephan said to Star, "I want to talk to you."

They sat in the den and Stephan said to her, "I've decided that I'm going to trust you and Rudy. I talked to Inez and she seems to think he can be trusted. I also talked to Norma. She told me I can trust you too."

"Trust me—what do you think we're going to do?"

Stephan didn't answer.

"Dad, don't worry, I'm not going to sleep with Rudy. I trust him too." She moved over and sat next to him, put her arms around him, and kissed him on the cheek. "Dad I love you so much."

That night she called Rudy to give him the good news. When Rudy got to Star's house, Stephan had already left to pick up Norma. As soon as Star saw Rudy, she knew he had something serious on his mind.

"Is something wrong, Rudy?"

$\mathcal{R}$udy put his hands on her shoulders and drew her to him and kissed her.

"I've been thinking a lot about us, about our future. Star, I want you to marry me."

"What? Rudy, I can't? You know I'm only seventeen. My dad would never allow it."

"I didn't mean right now. What I meant was I want you to marry me as soon as you graduate in June. You'll be eighteen then. Don't say anything yet, let me finish.

"I'm going to the village where my grandfather lives in June. I'm going to spend six months there helping the people that live in the village build a better school and a few homes. Star, I want you to go with me. My grandfather's going to love you. He can teach you what he knows about healing and how to work with herbs and whatever else you want to know."

"Rudy, everything is happening so fast and so soon."

"You love me, don't you?"

"Yes, you know I love you."

"Then that's all that matters."

"We don't have to mention any of this to our parents until a couple of months before you graduate. I'll tell my parents about my plans now. That will give my father a chance to get over the fit he's going to have—when I tell him I'm going to Mexico to help my grandfather's people."

"All right, yes, I'll marry you, Rudy."

"I love you, Star, I'll always take care of you."

"I'll always love you, my prince."

They embraced, kissed, and shut out the world.

Then they heard someone clearing their throat. It was Inez.

"Excuse me, I thought you two might want to come into the den and sit down. I can bring you some sodas to drink if you want."

They looked at each other, a little embarrassed. Star said. "Sure, why not. Thanks Inez."

"Do you think she heard us talking?" asked Rudy. When Inez had gone.

"I don't think so; at least I hope she didn't. If she did, she'll tell me as soon as you leave."

As soon as Rudy left, Inez came out of the kitchen. "Star, I told you I trusted the boy. Don't make me take those words back."

"Inez, all we were doing was kissing."

"That was some kiss."

"I love him, Inez."

"Oh *meja,* you're so young."

"I've already heard it all from my dad."

"All right, I've said my piece." She shot Star a warning look.

Rudy called Star. He wanted her to meet his parents before he went back to San Francisco.

"Meet your parents," said Star. "After what you told me about your father, you want me to go and meet him?"

"Forget about my father. It's my mother I really want you to meet. She will love you as much as I do."

"Are you sure about that?"

"Yes, I'm sure. I'll pick you up Saturday about six. Is that okay?"

"Sure, I'll be ready."

When Rudy and Star drove up to his parents' home, she wasn't prepared to see such a big and beautiful house. Compared to her home, this was almost a mansion. Her hands were wet with perspiration, she was so nervous.

As soon as they walked in his mother immediately greeted them. She had on a blue sundress that went a little past her knees and a light-blue vest. She was a pretty woman with green eyes and a wonderful smile. She had short strawberry blond hair. It was easy to see where Rudy got his green eyes. He hugged his mother and kissed her on the cheek.

"Mom, I want you to meet my girlfriend, Star Serban. Star, this is my mother, Patricia."

"Oh, Rudy, don't be so formal. Call me Pat. You know, Star, you're the first girl Rudy has ever brought home for us to meet. I can see why." She looked at Rudy and said, "She's lovely, son."

Just then his father walked in. Raymond Linarez was a big, handsome man, but at the same time he looked very intimidating.

He Nodded at Rudy. "And who is this?"

"You know very well who this is, Father."

Raymond just stared at Rudy.

Just then the cook announced that dinner was served. Pat said, "Wonderful. You come with me, Star." She made sure that Star wasn't seated next to Raymond.

Right off, Raymond started asking Star questions, such as why her father would allow her to date someone four years older than she. Star simply answered. "Because he trusts me and he trusts Rudy."

Before he opened his mouth again, Pat said. "Our son has brought his girlfriend to meet us and to have a nice dinner with us. Not to be interrogated by you. If you can't say anything nice, don't say anything at all." Raymond stood up, threw his napkin on the table, turned, and walked out of the dining room.

Pat said. "Well now we can eat in peace. Sorry about that, Star. If you keep on dating Rudy, you'll just have to learn how to ignore Raymond."

By the time they left Rudy's parents' house, Star didn't know what to think about them. Rudy said, "And you thought your family was weird."

"Why does your mom stay with him?"

"I don't know. I suppose she's used to him, or she loves him no matter what. You know what they say, love is blind. Don't worry about my mom; she can take care of herself."

It was the weekend that Rudy was going back to San Francisco. Seven more months, thought Star and she would be eighteen. She could marry Rudy any time after that. She hadn't gone up to the attic since Rudy had come home. Once Rudy was gone, she would spend as much time as she could in the attic reading the books on how to cure with herbs and flowers.

The big book fascinated her. She knew she couldn't take it out of the house. The best thing she could do was write down some of the spells and cures so that she could show them to Rudy's grandfather once they arrived in Mexico.

Rudy left for San Francisco, and Stephan was relieved. In his imagination Rudy would meet an older girl in San Francisco. He would break Star's heart, but she would get over it and move on. After all, she was only seventeen years old.

Poor Stephan. If he only knew what those two were planning.

The only one who knew was Inez, and only because of her eavesdropping, but she wasn't about to say anything. Star went back to her old routine of school, work, and the attic. She tried to read as many books as she could; she also took a lot of notes. She wanted to take as much information as possible to show to Rudy's grandfather. She had a feeling that if anyone could teach her what she had to learn, he would be the one. Rudy would only have to interrupt a little; thanks to Inez, she knew some Spanish.

It was almost Christmas, and Rudy would be home for two weeks. At breakfast a couple of days before Rudy was due back.

Star said to Stephan, "Dad, Rudy's coming home for two weeks. Please be nice when he comes to see me."

"You two are still going together?"

"Yes Dad. Did you think just because he wasn't around, we had broken up?"

"I didn't say that."

But he secretly hoped that's what had happened.

"Star I'm always nice, you know that."

"Sure, you are, at least you're nicer than his father."

"Why? What happened?"

"Before Rudy left in September he took me to his house so I could meet his parents. Rudy especially wanted me to meet his mother, but his father was really rude at the dinner table. He ended up leaving without even eating his dinner. His mother was really nice I liked her a lot."

"Raymond was always a hothead, I should talk to him."

"No Dad it would just make things worse, he might take it out on Rudy."

"All right, but if he's ever rude to you again I want you to tell me, you hear me Star?"

"All right Dad I will."

Inez came in after breakfast and announced that a letter had arrived from a Mrs. Marie Ann O'Neal. Star ran and practically grabbed the letter out of her hand.

"Dad!" she yelled. "Here's a letter from Marie Ann." She opened the letter. "Look, she sent pictures of the wedding. She says that she apologizes for taking so long in sending them. She says that she's been very busy working with Patrick's mother at the tackle shop. When she gets home she's busy fixing up their new little cottage. She also has to have dinner ready for Patrick when he gets home from working with the tourists on the boats all day. She says it's a lot of work, but she loves it. She loves Patrick more and more every day. "PS. I love you all and think about you all the time. I miss my grandma. Please look in on her from time to time for me. Thanks, all my love, Marie Ann."

"Well I'm glad our girl is happy," said Stephan. "Maybe someday we'll take a plane and go and visit them."

"That would be nice. I still miss her lot, Dad."

"I know, honey, we all do, but I know you do most of all."

"Oh Dad, I'm going out with Rudy tonight. He's taking me out to dinner."

"Why don't you two have dinner here?"

"Dad!" "All right, all right."

At dinner Rudy fidgeted nervously with his silverware. He drank his glass of water in one gulp.

"Rudy," said Star, "is something wrong?"

"No, there's nothing wrong, why?"

"You seem awfully nervous."

"There is something I want to ask you, Star."

"What is it? Just ask me."

He reached in his pocket and took out a small box. "I know that you already agreed to marry me, but I thought you should have a ring. Right now I can't afford to buy you a diamond ring." He held out the box. "This was my grandmother's wedding ring. My grandfather gave it to me to give to the women I would marry. Will you accept it, Star?"

Star opened the box and smiled. "Rudy it's beautiful."

"Really? I wasn't sure if you would like it. The stone is a tiger's eye. It's thought to be a very powerful protective stone. It enhances courage and mental clarity. The carvings are ancient Mayan."

"Why wasn't it passed on to your mother?"

"My father didn't want it. He bought my mother a big diamond ring."

"I don't need a diamond. I love this one."

Rudy went back to San Francisco. Star hid her ring; she didn't want a scene with her dad until it was absolutely necessary. She had to have someone to talk to and Marie Ann was in Ireland. The only one she could talk to was Norma. Inez still thought of her as her *little Mejita.*(*Her little girl.*)Not as someone that was almost a women.

It was already February and Star had made up her mind she wanted to marry Rudy in the spring, as soon as she turned eighteen. She wanted their wedding on the beach during the spring equinox. She had already talked to Rudy about it. He said, "Whatever you want, Star, as long as we get married."

Star told Norma she wanted to talk to her about something personal after everyone left the shop for the day.

"What is it Star. Is something wrong?"

"Well, yes and no. You know that I've been going with Rudy Linarez since Uncle Duncan and Renee's wedding."

"I knew you were going with him when you mentioned it to me some time ago. I also had a discussion about it with your dad.

Star, I had no idea you had been seeing Rudy since the wedding. My goodness, that's been a long time. How did you keep it from your dad until now?"

"He goes to college in San Francisco, so I didn't get to see him very often. I talk to him on the phone every day, and he comes home on holidays."

"What's the problem, Star?"

"Well, first my dad's not too pleased that he's my boy-friend; he says he's too old for me. But Norma, I'm going to be eighteen in April, and I love Rudy and he loves me. Rudy's going to Mexico in June to help his grandfather's people build a school and some homes. I'm going with him, Norma."

"Have you told your dad?"

"No. I'm going right after I graduate."

"I don't know what to tell you, Star, except that your dad's not going to be happy about the whole thing."

"I know, Norma. I love my dad and I don't want to hurt him, but I have to do this. That's not all. Rudy and I want to get married before we go to Mexico."

"Star, are you sure? You're so young. You'll barely be eighteen."

"Norma, we love each other."

119

"Star, I know what first love feels like, but sometimes it doesn't last."

"We'll never know if we don't take a chance."

"How long do you plan to be in Mexico?"

"Only for six months. After that we'll be back. I plan to go to nursing school as soon as we get back. Rudy has already been promised a job when we get back."

"Well, you two seem to have everything all thought out."

"Can I ask you for a favor, Norma? Will you try to calm my dad down after I tell him? I know he's going to tell you all about it."

"I will if he brings it up."

"Thanks, Norma. I really appreciate it."

For two nights, Star worried and paced up and down in her room, almost wearing a hole in the carpet. How was she going to bring up the subject to her dad? Should she butter him up first and then say, *Dad, Rudy and I are getting married?* She grabbed her pendant and made a wish, that things would work out and her dad would be okay with her and Rudy's plans.

After dinner, Stephan seemed to be in a good mood. Star asked him, "What's going on Dad?"

"I feel pretty good," said Stephan. "Things at the office are going great, and we just won a big case. I have my beautiful girl here and a great girlfriend. What more can a man ask for?"

Star thought to herself, *that's just great.* She hadn't seen him this happy in a long time. Maybe she should put off their talk for later, but later he would still be happy.

"Dad, I have something to talk to you about."

"What is it, honey?"

"First, I want you to know that I love you very much and that I know you spend your life taking care of me. That I was your first priority, and I will never forget it."

"Okay, Star, now you're scaring me."

Meanwhile Inez was listening to every word from the kitchen.

"Dad, please don't say anything until I'm finished talking. Then you can scream at me."

"Star!"

"Dad, Rudy is going to Mexico in June to help his grandfather's people build a school and a few homes. He asked me to marry him and go with him to Mexico for six months. When we get back, I'm going to enroll in nursing school, and Rudy already has a job promised to him when we get back."

Stephan just sat there for what seemed like forever.

"Dad? Say something?"

"What can I say, Star? Apparently you and Rudy have thought of everything. I can't stop you unless I lock you in the attic or tie you in a chair in your room. What I'm trying to say is that I knew this day would come, but I never thought it would come this soon. All right, Star, do what you have to do, and may God protect you both."

"Dad I love you!" She flung her arms around him and kissed him. "I'm going upstairs to call Rudy. Dad, I love you."

Inez walked in and found Stephan with tears in his eyes.

"You heard everything?" he said.

"Yes, but they'll be back in six months. We haven't lost our little girl. Anyway you have Norma. She loves you, don't you know?"

"Is there anything you don't know, Inez?"

"Not much." She laughed and walked away.

In April, the weekend after Star turned eighteen, she had the wedding of her dreams. With the help of Renee, Norma, and Rudy's mother, she walked down the aisle on the beach after sunset. There was a full moon; the sky was covered with stars that looked like crystals illuminating the night sky, just like she had dreamed.

On each side of the aisle there were twenty white wooden chairs decorated with green ferns. White torches wrapped in ferns and cherry blossoms led the way to the wedding arbor, which was decorated with gardenias. The floor of the aisle was covered with pink rose petals. Star wore the crescent-moon pendant and her great grandmother's wedding dress, thanks to Renee, who had it altered for her. Norma styled her hair beautifully, and she carried a bouquet of white lilacs.

As Stephan walked her down the aisle, he looked up and saw a star streaking across the sky, just like the night she was born. He smiled; he knew then that his little girl would be all right. Music played their favorite love song. "Love at first sight, by "The Maulin Rouge." After Rudy and Star said their marriage vows to each other, they kissed, (which may have been the sweetest and longest kiss ever.)

The reception was held on the beach. Inez was responsible for the wedding cake. Star was glad to see her dad looking happy. That made Star feel good. She hoped that he and Norma would get more serious with each other.

Rudy went back to college until the second week of June.

Star went back to school; she also continued working at Norma's.

She gathered all the information and books from the attic she was going to take to Mexico with her. She was so anxious for Rudy to come home that she was packed a couple of weeks ahead of time.

A week after she graduated from high school, Rudy came to pick her up. She was already packed and ready for her trip to Mexico. She had already put her suitcases outside of her bedroom door when she hesitated. She went back in and opened the closet door, picked up the teapot, put it in her suitcase, and closed the door.

About The Author

This is the second book Emily Del Rosario's has published, but her first fiction book. Emily lives with her husband on a ranch in the small community of Selma, Oregon.

Emily is a traveler who has spent time visiting many of the states in the US, as well as Egypt, Costa Rica, Honduras, Guatemala and many places in the Caribbean. Her favorite place is Yucatan, Mexico.

She loves talking and learning as much as she can about the countries she visits and their people.

$\mathcal{E}$ mily Del Rosario dedicates this book to all the young adults who love romance and the paranormal.

An infant girl was born during the "Spring Equinox." As the years went by she began to notice that she was different from the other children in school. Her father hid the truth from her thinking she was too young to know she had the power of premonition.

He also asked her, to never go into the attic in their home. As a teen, Star also kept her own secrets from her father. The biggest secret was when she falls in love. She hides that fact from everyone except her best friend Marie Ann.